The Blood of Life

NightEyes DaySpring

Dancing Jackal Books

For Othello, who keeps me on track.

Content Warning:

The following work contains scenes of explicit male/ male sex and includes descriptions of violence and death. This book is intended for adults only, and reader discretion is advised.

Table of Contents

The Twilight of Life.. 1
The Twisted Vines of the Past 5
A Rest Interrupted 17
The Seduction of Loneliness... 29
A False Dawn... 47
Eternal Dusk 59
The Lonely Hunt 73
The Moon's Touch... 85
As the Night Darkened 97
Embers of the Fire 109
Whispers of the Past 119
Ties of Blood 131
The Last Sunset... 155
Hunters in the Night... 175
The Rites of Death 185
The Embrace of Eternity.. 195

Afterword.. 217
About the Author 219

The Twilight of Life

My footpaws sink into the grass of the cemetery. As I follow the priest carrying a lantern through the dark, I can feel the connection to the earth within myself. It is spring, the insects sing of the coming summer, and the trees are alive with new growth after their long winter slumber, and yet I find myself among the dead in the cool night air. I'm not sure I should have come, but I had to return to finally pay my respects.

It's been a hundred years since that night, but I remember it as if it was only yesterday. The fangs that sunk into my neck and stole my life away are forever burned into my mind. I cannot forget that moment, that feeling of helplessness. I was his prey, and nothing more. To him, I was a vessel to be drunk till it was dry and tossed aside, unwanted and unneeded. He cared not for what happened to me afterward, even though he must have known what his curse could do.

He was sloppy. I don't know what happened to him, but I never saw him again. Someone must have found him and staked him. As for me, he left me where I fell by the side of the road. Whoever buried my lifeless body didn't do their job right and perform the rituals to stop the curse, because the cemetery is where I found myself when I awoke the next night—hungry, desperate to feed, and forever changed. The first ten years were hell as the hunger ripped at me, and I did things that left stains on my soul I will never be able to wash away. The next ninety were a miserable suffering spent working to gain control of myself, trying to understand who I had become.

The lupine priest stops at the plot of graves we'd been looking for, and I kneel down in the grass in front of the stone that guards my secret. I reach out to touch it, to feel its coolness in the night against the paw pads of my handpaw.

One would think that in a hundred years someone would have realized something was amiss and dug up the plot, but I guess when everyone you know dies, there's no one left to ask questions. Maybe my parents didn't believe it when the gravediggers told them that my grave had been disturbed and the body was missing. I know my escape from the coffin required me to claw my way to the surface, yet the headstone is still here. Maybe they knew I would someday need closure.

"Was he a relative of yours?" asks the priest, breaking the silence. He lifts the lantern and watches me patiently. I'm surprised that this is the first question he's asked me about why I'm visiting his church's graveyard after nightfall.

"You could say that," I say, running my black-furred digits across my name, Radic Horban. "I owe him my life."

"I heard he died suddenly. Violently," says the priest.

"He did."

The priest comes closer and places a handpaw on my shoulder. "You should come to the chapel and pray, my son."

"I can't, Father." I look up at the old wolf in his vestments looking down at me. "I just can't, but if you could say a few words for him, and all of his family, I'd appreciate it."

"Of course, I'd be happy to. The family were all red foxes, like you?" he asks.

My voice catches just a little. "Yes indeed."

For his part, the priest does not seem bothered by any of this but has taken to seeing me through. Maybe he knows who I really am; maybe he doesn't. I don't plan to stay long enough here for it to matter. He doesn't ask why a fox in his late twenties is pining over tombstones for people who died long before he should have been born. He doesn't remark that I share the same first name as the one on the headstone. Instead, he says a blessing and reads by lantern light from a prayer book. He prays for the souls of my parents, my sister, and me. I mouth the words with him and bow my head.

When he's done, he looks at me. "Peace be upon you," he says.

"And to you," I say, "and thank you for this. I'd like to be alone now."

The priest nods and walks back to the church and the rectory, carrying his lantern.

When he's gone, and I'm alone in the darkness, I finally let myself cry. Tears of blood drip onto the ground. I never did find out the name of the man who cursed me, but I wish I had. I'd have sent him to hell if I could, but it's been too long to be angry anymore. Now I just have sadness, and a dull ache from hunger I can never truly satisfy. The need for blood is always with me, but right now … I want to pretend I'm still normal.

Tonight, I choose to starve.

The Twisted Vines of the Past

It amazes me that even after all these years, Strasek still looks like the village I remember. So much has changed since the wars of Napoleon and the recent revolutions, and yet it seems as though time has moved more slowly here. Great battles have been fought, nations have come and gone, but here in the foothills of the Carpathian Mountains, surrounded by vineyards and fields of grain, there is a feeling of peace — as if this area had simply opted out of the growing march of steam-driven progress engulfing other parts of Europe, and existed only to watch the world beyond.

Perhaps it will catch up when the railroads reach Strasek and link it to the rest of the empire. Factories bring opportunity, but they also bring the choking darkness of smog. So far, the changes I have noticed around town on my trip seem to suggest a sense of refinement instead of a sense of progress. New houses have been built over the intervening years and familiar buildings have been modified with new wings added, yet they form a cohesive whole. Other things are still the same. The Twisted Vine remains the only lodgings in town, standing just off the main square, although it too has gained an addition and been remodeled inside.

This village was my home, but it's not my home anymore. I'm reminded of that strolling down the dirt lane in front of my parents' house. It doesn't look like it's been altered much, just like the rest of Strasek around it, but it looks like the wealth of the occupants has faded with time. The roof sags in spots, and the paint has peeled. I've yet to determine if it's still owned by any of my relatives. My sister Katarina had a kit, Gavrilo, but I have no idea if he lived to adulthood. He was four at the time of my attack. Since there is no tombstone for him in the family plot, I can only assume he did, but I have no idea where he ended up.

All I have here now are memories, and as I walk back to The Twisted Vine, I can feel a pinprick of uncertainty. This is where I met the man who turned me. I had serious trepidation when I arrived in town yesterday, since I was once again bringing my corruption among the living, but I had to if I was going to finally do this. I needed to finally say goodbye.

So far, the innkeeper Alina hasn't shown any suspicions of who I or what I am, which is good. The response to my letter asking about accommodations invited me to visit, so I had no problem entering when I arrived. It proved to be a welcoming place, and returning to the tavern, I can feel the life and joy the building contains. It is warm and homey; a fire burns in the fireplace with oil lamps lighting the rest of the room. Alina immediately waves to me from the bar. Even though the badger is tending to some drinkware, she stops to check on me.

"Good evening, Master Radic. Will you be taking your meal in your room again tonight?" she asks me so warmly, that for a moment, I think she might be a child of the sun. She would not be so welcoming if she knew the danger of the guest before her.

I smile, trying to return some of the warmth from my cold, dead body. "My stomach is still bothering me," I respond, approaching the counter, "but if you'd send up some wine and bread, I'd be quite thankful for it." The bread at least has a pleasant smell about it, and while I can't eat it, I could at least enjoy the scent before I would have to find a way to get rid of it. The wine is something I can handle.

"You sure a good stew wouldn't set you right, sir?"

"I'm sure, but thank you for offering."

"Suit yourself. Did the walk at least help you feel better?"

"That it did."

She is pleased about that, at least. "Oh good. I was worried you would be ill since you slept so late."

I nod. "I was tired from the road, and I am quite the night owl."

"Aye, well you let me know if you need anything," she says.

I nod in agreement again and turn toward the stairs. The inn is busy, and the fire down here is warm, but I know my place is not here. I'm almost to the stairs in the back when a friendly handpaw waves me down.

"Radic, please join me again tonight," calls out a leopard.

It is Ekrem, a man I met last night here in the common room. He is taking his evening meal by himself at a table here by the stairs. I consider for a moment, pondering if I want to stay downstairs, but it won't hurt. Even though I plan to leave tomorrow night, it would be good to keep people reassured. Plus, he's easy on the eyes.

"If you insist," I say, approaching, "but I wouldn't want to impose."

"Please," he says, pointing to the chair in front of me. "I do insist. You came a long way and just left the world of the dead. I wouldn't want you to think Strasek is only for the deceased."

I chuckle and take my seat. "Thank you, but my concern isn't with the living right now."

"I have not forgotten. Your meeting with the priest went well?" he asks.

"It did. Thank you for arranging that for me and delivering my note. I needed the rest after getting in so late."

He nods. "You're welcome. Does that conclude your business in town?"

"It does provide some closure. I've done what I came here to do."

"Will you be leaving soon then?" asks the leopard. He looks a little disappointed I'll be going.

"In a few days, I plan to head back to Vienna."

His ears dip. "Quite an awfully long trip to just visit some graves."

I shrug. It isn't his business, but I don't want to arouse any undue suspicion. "It was a promise kept."

"A strange promise," he remarks.

"People ask for strange things on their deathbeds, sometimes. She wanted me to visit them, and I did." I repeat the lie I told him last night about my odd request.

"I am sorry for your loss."

"Thank you. What about you? Business was good today?"

"It was slow, but I made a few guldens."

Alina comes over and drops off the wine and bread I asked for, along with two goblets. I thank her, but I wish she hadn't brought it to me. This means I will have to keep up the act about my stomach in front of the leopard.

"A light dinner, I see," Ekrem says.

"My stomach has been bothering me," I respond, reaching for the wine and pulling the cork to let the contents breathe. The heady scent tickles my nose; oh good, it's a red wine. That agrees with me more than white wines do.

"Ah, I did not know," he says.

"It happens when I travel. Hopefully tomorrow it will be settled."

"Indeed. You must have some of Alina's cooking. It is quite good."

Looking at the stew, I want to agree. I would love to tuck into a meal like that right now. The bowl of beef and vegetables looks hearty, comforting, and above all similar to what my mother used to make. It is a meal to help warm your tired body during cold nights. Oh, how I miss the true pleasures of life.

My ears must show my disappointment, because Ekrem speaks up. "I can give you a bite."

I shake my head and reach for the wine, pouring some out into the simple glass goblet the innkeeper placed on the table. "I'll be okay."

The leopard shrugs and dips his spoon into the stew to take another bite. The smell is quite delightful, and I can at least remember what food was like. The company is pleasant, and as we talk, I offer him some of the bread, which he accepts gratefully. For my part, I sit and slowly sip my wine.

"I must ask," he says when the meal is finished, "have you heard of the legend about Strasek's greatest defender?"

My ears perk. I have, but it would be good to hear it again. "I did hear a story about that before, but I'm not sure it's the same one you know."

He smiles. "I can tell you the version I know then."

I lift my glass and take a sip. "Go on. I'm interested."

Ekrem clears his throat. "Our town is a sleepy place, but it has not always been that way. The wars of the previous centuries thundered across these lands, and many of the people here suffered. It was said there was a bear who stood up and fought year after year against those who would do the village and the surrounding countryside harm. Some say he fought the Turks, others the Russians. There are some who say he was so old he even fought the Huns, but who would believe such nonsense? A few people believe he actually fought them all and that he survived just to fight, for he had nothing left to him but to fight. When a war was over, he would vanish, only to reappear when the village was again threatened. Always he would strike from the woods and subsequently disappear back into them."

"That's the legend of the Huntsman. That story is old, and even I know that."

Ekrem chuckles. "It is, but do you know how they say the Huntsman died?"

I shake my head. "No, I don't." This part was never in any of the stories I had heard growing up.

"About a hundred years ago, there was a man who came to Strasek who had heard of the Huntsman, and he came seeking not to fight him or to aid him but to take his power. He came and he waited for a war to come, but none did, so he searched the woods around Strasek for years, seeking the Huntsman. They say deep in the forest he found him, and they fought. This man bested the Huntsman and drank the old bear's blood to capture his power, but it did not make him stronger. Instead, it drove him mad. Where the Huntsman was kind, he became cruel and had no noble traits like the Huntsman. He craved only flesh after that, and he struck the village of Strasek with his evil before he was driven off. Since that time the man and the Huntsman have not been seen, and if the legend is true, the Huntsman will never return again."

I sit in silence, nervous about the implications behind the story. "What of the man's victims?"

"The stories don't say, but it is rumored the man became cursed with a hunger he could never sate. He left Strasek, but if he became one with death like that, he might still be out there."

I take a sip of my wine, trying not to show my unease. "Indeed, he might."

The leopard smiles. "It is a legend of course, but be careful, my friend, if you choose to travel the mountain roads at night."

"I think I'll be okay," I say before I flash my fangs. "I would not be an easy prey for a robber."

He sits back and drums his digits against the wooden table. "Perhaps," he says, "but who knows what stalks the night."

I lift up my glass again. "Indeed, who knows."

"You're an odd man, Radic, traveling all this way to pay respect to the dead. I sense there is great sadness in you but also something special. Something that sets you apart."

I almost choke on my wine. I must clear my throat before I can speak. "I am but a traveler in this world. An observer, if you might say." I hope my hackles aren't coming up.

Ekrem flicks an ear before he responds. "A good traveler is always watching the road and the people around him. On this note, tell me about Vienna," he asks. "I've never been, and I hear the city brims with wealth, and its streets are lit at night with so many gas lights that the city twinkles in the darkness."

"It most certainly does." I put the goblet down on the worn wooden table, thinking. "It's a city full of life, and the promise of what tomorrow will bring. There is wondrous music that fills the city's ballrooms with guests waltzing until late into the night. Vienna's artists and opera singers rival the best found in Paris."

He reaches toward my handpaw holding the goblet, and his digits wrap around mine. "I don't know when I will be able to make a trip there myself, so I'd like to hear about it."

I look down at the paw on top of mine. If he was trying to sniff out my secret, why is he suddenly trying to reassure me? "I wouldn't want to bore you," I offer.

He gently squeezes my handpaw. "You wouldn't. Also, you are cold, would you like to sit by the fire? It seems you caught a chill out there."

I look up at the leopard and see his eyes have become saucer like. He does seem really interested in what I have to say, and I smile. A genuine smile. This isn't the one I gave Alina, but something warmer—something almost alive. "Let us sit by the fire, and I would be happy to tell you what it's like in Vienna."

☘

It is well after midnight when I finally take the time to pause my reading. I have heard no movement downstairs for a while, and I stop, letting my ears swivel to see if they pick up anything.

All is silent. I cannot be sure, but I think everyone has gone to bed now, resting from the day. I know when Ekrem and I parted earlier tonight, the tavern was almost empty. Only the most nocturnal are awake right now. I include myself in that, but I am awake every night and have been for a hundred years. This is my day.

I place the book down on the table and get up silently to stretch, waking my stiff muscles. There is a familiar itch under my fur, and it is best to scratch it. I still need to let myself pretend I am alive for at least another day, before I take my leave of Strasek tomorrow.

First, I strip off my clothing, folding it up to the side. Then, I carefully snuff out the few candles in the room I have lit, plunging the space into near total darkness. I have let the fire in the fireplace burn down, so it gives off only a faint orange glow from the remaining embers. The distinct scent of extinguished, wax-fed flames hangs in the air as I step over to the window and slowly open it.

The night air is cool and quickly washes away the lingering smoke as I push out the shutters. Moonlight falls over me, bathing me in its silvery light. The village is quiet, and most of the people should be asleep. My room looks over the back of the inn and the yard behind it. I still myself and look up at the moon to focus on it, and suddenly I am no longer myself.

The change is instant, and even though I've gone through the process enough times for it to be effortless, there's still a joy about it. The feeling of freedom it gives as I beat my wings to get air under them never gets old. As I push myself out of the open window, the world below me spirals away. It is a thing full of moonlight and shadows.

As I stretch out my wings and swoop across the yard and over the buildings below, I can see that my assumptions about everyone being asleep are correct. Few lights are lit in the town, and only a little smoke is coming out of the chimneys. In Vienna, there are always people awake doing something, and I need to be cautious in my nocturnal wanderings, but here? It doesn't feel like there's much danger of someone happening upon my small and innocuous presence at all. And indeed, what harm does a little bat present to them if they don't know the monster it can be?

The curse that binds me to the dark also lets me see the world like I never could before, and the simple joy of flying almost lets me forget what cost I paid for this ability. I easily take in the whole village, flying in large, sweeping circles over it. The street layout is still familiar, and the central square is still like I remember it. The stores have changed, but that's to be expected. The only light in the center of town comes from the rooms above the curiosity shop, which is where my dinner companion lives. Something must have caught Ekrem's attention, or perhaps the stew didn't agree with him.

I push myself higher, letting my concern for the leopard fall behind me. He is better with me far away from him. He has his life and store, and I have my undeath back in Vienna.

Such is the way of the world and the things that could have been but can't be. I must drink in the beauty of Strasek tonight, and only tonight, before it becomes another faded memory for me.

The hunger still burns inside of me, but it is forgotten as I let the feeling of the wind and the freedom it brings fill me. I have long missed the sun, but this is one thing the curse has given me that I can appreciate. Suspended in the moonlight of the night, I can forget my fears, my problems, and my hunger.

The village disappears as I let my wings carry me away. Fields filled with ripening winter grain and grapes cover the hills below me. They stretch all the way to the nearby mountains. I swing down to catch the scents and let myself skim just over the sheaves of wheat, as I head toward a farmhouse.

Silently I reach the structure and catch my tiny claws into the wood of the eaves. I hang there for a moment, letting myself rest. The gentle sound of snoring comes to my ears. Entry is impossible due to the bindings against me the curse imposes, but it would be no trouble to draw the farmer and his wife out by making a disturbance. The meal would be quick, and if I played my cards right, I might get both of them. It would invigorate me and give me the strength I need to make the journey back to Vienna.

Except I can't. Not now, and not ever again. I swore to myself I wouldn't ever feed like that, and I won't break that oath. I turn my head to look over the fields. This is a village of light and hope. It does not suffer under the industrial might of the empire like some places now do. I will not sully such a beautiful place with my presence longer than I must.

I stretch out my wings and let go, gliding away from the house before I start to beat them. Strasek deserves better than me in its midst. It is still a few hours till dawn, but I cannot let myself dawdle out here too long. Before the night is done, I need to secure some fresh dirt from the graveyard. It will ease my mind and let me sleep well. It has been difficult to get a good rest on this trip, so it will be blissful to sleep deeply. Tomorrow I will arrange to have my trunk sent off and head by wing to the cave I stayed at on my last night before reaching here. I stashed some clothing there, so if I leave a note saying I left before dawn, no one will know I am sending my clothing back to Vienna in the trunk.

Tomorrow I will feed on some cattle before I head to the cave. I will leave the village of my birth behind, safe in my past. None will suspect a thing except Ekrem, and he will know me as only a traveler full of stories of places far from here. That's what I want.

A Rest Interrupted

The sound of someone knocking awakens me with a start. I am lying nude on the bed, on top of some graveyard dirt. It's not a proper resting place with the meager amount of dirt I have, but I was sleeping deeply this time. The extra sack of soil I secured this morning before dawn had eased my rest. Through the heavy curtain over the window, I can see a faint glow that hurts my eyes. It's not bright enough in here to be a danger to me, but I do wish the room was darker.

The knocking continues. "Radic," I hear through the door. Quickly I scramble up. "I found something, Radic."

It's that leopard from last night. Why is Ekrem here, and what time is it anyway? I fumble for the pocket watch on the nightstand, which I click open. Foxes have good night vision, and by the faint light in the room, I can just barely make out that it is only 10:30 in the morning. I am a prisoner in here.

"Radic?" calls the voice. "Are you awake?"

"I am now," I snap, immediately regretting my outburst. He's going to expect me to open the door, and I can't do that. I look back to the bed and my makeshift coffin with dirt sitting on top of a blanket. He's going to have questions.

"Alina says you sleep pretty late, but this is important. I was going through things at the store after our chat, and I found something you are going to want to see."

"I'm not decent right now, Ekrem. Could we perhaps talk about this tonight?" What is he doing here? I can't let him in, but if I don't let him in, that's going to be suspicious.

There's a pause. "I think you will want to see this now."

I take a deep sigh. Once again, people won't leave me alone. I came here to seek solitude, but life has apparently found me.

"Radic?" There's hesitation in his voice now. Confusion. Maybe he's going to get someone else. No, there's no time to wait. I must handle the problem in front of me and see if I can buy time to think.

I walk over to the door and slide the bolt open. I take a deep breath, and plan to just tell him politely that we can talk later. I crack the door open and lean to stick my muzzle out the door when the light from the window in the hallway burns my nose with indirect daylight.

Immediately, I fall back. Even though it's not directly on my face, I can feel the sudden pain. In that moment, as I hiss at my own stupidity, I can feel the door bump me as he enters the room.

I freeze then. It's been decades since I've consumed blood from sapient life, and I did not plan to ever do it again, but he has forced my hand. I either take care of him, or my secret is going to be exposed.

"I didn't want to do this," I say, straightening up and pushing the door closed, "but you couldn't leave me alone."

He looks at me. "Oh wow, you are ... naked."

"Yes," I hiss. Maybe if I physically knock him out, no one will come looking for him till dark. It's a risk, but it's better than killing him. I just can't let there be a struggle.

"Also, it's quite dark in here. Here, let me get the window for you— "

"No!" I shout, and he freezes. For a moment we appraise each other. His eyes glance toward the bed, but I try and place myself between him and it. "What do you want?"

He looks me over, and even though he is little more than an outline in the darkened room, I can see his tail has gone still. He's realized what the mess on the bed means. "That family plot you visited last night…"

"What about it?" I snap.

He looks at me, and I can smell fear. "That's where you were buried, isn't it," he whispers.

With a sinking feeling, I give a small nod and reach over to slide the bolt of the door closed. After so long, I thought the nightmare of who I am was over for me. "I'm sorry for what I'm about to do to you," I say, taking a step toward him. I can feel my fangs starting to extend. "I can't afford you telling anyone."

He swallows. "I found the diary of Katarina Horban. There's a letter in it, and it appears to be addressed to you."

I freeze, body tense and coiled, ready to take him out as quickly as I can. "Katarina…" I whisper.

The leopard nods. "She was your sister?" he asks.

I should kill him. It would be quick and bloody, but it would be easy. The blood in his body taunts me, calling out to me. It could all be mine. I would again feel the true power my curse gives me, and I would once again be drunk on the power of death.

I don't want to have to throw out ninety years of fighting back against myself for one curious leopard. I settle my fur down and study him, as best I can in the darkness. I didn't come here to run from the past. I've done that for a long time. I came here to face it and put it behind me. To once more know the thoughts of my sister is a temptation greater than blood.

Now that I'm looking at him as more than just a problem I need to kill, I can see the leopard is dressed in simple clothes, but he is carrying a book under one arm. It's a sharp contrast to the naked, dirt-smudged fox standing in front of him with clumps of earth stuck to his fur.

"Don't make me regret this," I say, putting as much ice in my voice I can. It's a half-hearted threat. My choice of diet has taken away my powers of suggestion. There's something that the blood of intelligent creatures gives you that the blood of simple farm animals can't. Who knew that I would lose one of the core ways I had to protect myself when I stopped feeding on innocents?

Ekrem, for his part, just slowly holds up the book. There is a piece of paper sticking out of it.

I take the book, and it feels familiar. It is warm in my handpaws because he was holding it. There are no words on the spine and the leather cover is much more worn since I last saw it sitting at her writing desk, but I recognize it. Eagerly, I flip it open, but it's too dark in the room for me to read the text.

Quickly, I walk over and strike a match to light the candle. Once it's lit, I open the book. The handwriting on the inside cover is Katarina's—it is indeed her diary. My paws are shaking as I unfold the letter. My name is clearly on it, and it is dated seventy years ago. Nervously I read it, the leopard next to me forgotten.

My Dearest Brother,

> *I have often wondered what has become of you, but I cannot say if you still walk this world. Perhaps you have joined the angels above or the demons below. No one in the village remembers the day after we buried you anymore, but I know what I saw. Time erases much, and yet if you still live, time for you has frozen.*

> *If these words should ever find you, know that even in my waning days, I have thought of you, and even with everything that happened, I realize you suffered more*

than anyone in this. If only I could see you once more and tell you that I have waited for your return, no matter what it might bring. Perhaps this is for the best though, and you have stayed away to protect us. If that is the case, I cannot blame you for your absence. I hope whatever fate is yours, should it be in front of you or behind you, be it a gentle fate.

With love, your faithful sister,
Katarina

I go and sit on the bed clutching the letter, even though there is still dirt on top of it. She remembered me. She knew I was not beyond hope. Had I known, I would have come back or at least written to say goodbye. Instead, I waited till no one could identify me; no one could know for sure who I was. I waited until I was nothing more than an inscription on a stone and a half-remembered story.

"Thank you," I whisper. I look up at the leopard. "This means a lot to me." I close my eyes, and I feel them wet.

"Is this why you're here?" Ekrem asks me.

I nod my head. "I came to finally say goodbye when I thought it would be safe. I never thought they would want me to return."

"Are you still going back to Vienna?"

I sniff, even though I no longer breathe. A useless biological response, but one I still haven't completely lost. "What is there here for me? Katarina hoped I would return, but she's been dead a long time." I look at the dirt on the blanket, which my tail rests on. "Fresh graveyard dirt, dug from the land of my ancestors? Hardly worth it. Plus, there is you. You know too much now. It is best you do not know more."

His tail flicks behind him. "That seems like a lonely existence."

"A long, lonely existence. I can't stay in one place too long before people become suspicious, and I need to stay ahead of the hunters that would seek me out."

"So, you just wander around?" he asks.

I blink to clear the bloody tears from my eyes so I can look at him clearly. This requires me wiping them with my handpaw, which stains the black fur red. "What else can I do? Does it look like I can hide who I am? The curse is always upon me. The hunger, the need to feed, it's always there. Look at me, truly look at me. I am a monster, Ekrem. There's no place for me among people like you."

Ekrem clears his throat. "Not naked like this."

Oh right, I'm still nude and covered in dirt. "Modesty is for people who have a social standing to lose."

"Yes, well, there's the sheet, and the dirt, and the darkness. It's a bit primal."

"We're all animals in the end, fighting to survive. I thought myself different once, but my life has shown me how wrong that is," I say, getting up and dusting myself off. "Now there is the matter of what I should do with you."

"I understand the desire to pay your respects. I would not deny you that."

"I appreciate the sympathy." A tickle in the back of my mind comes to me. Did I somehow seduce this man with my powers to control the living? No ... I can't have. I've lost that ability. Well, there's one way to test it. "Take your clothes off."

He blinks. "What? Why?"

I chuckle. "Just checking."

"Checking?"

Since I'm not murdering him, I should at least put some clothing on. People don't take you seriously when you're naked. "Making sure I did not somehow command you."

His ears flick back and he gets sheepish. "You can ... do that?"

I go over and retrieve a shirt. "It comes with the curse, but I can't. Not anymore."

"But if you could?"

"I could make you mine, lay you on this bed, and do what I wish to you. If I can bend your will to mine, you would willingly offer me everything, including every drop of your blood in your veins."

He rubs his neck.

"Ah, now you see, don't you?" I say, walking over to him. "You realize what I can do to you. It's why they hunt vampires. The hunger, it makes us uncontrollable."

He steps back.

"I don't drink from sapient creatures, not anymore."

"But you did?"

I nod and stretch out my arms. "Oh yes. The first ten years were rough. I did not understand what I'd become." He's looking at me, but it's not with fear in his eyes. I put my arms down. "I don't scare you?"

He shifts between paws. "Not exactly. You seem more misunderstood than anything else."

My muzzle hangs open, and there's nothing I can say to that.

"No one has told you that before?"

"Why would they?" I finally say. "Where did you get this anyway?" I ask, holding up the letter.

"Last night, when I went back to the shop, I was thinking, and I realized I had seen the surname Horban before. There are some items in the shop that have never sold, and I was looking through some of the old books in the back. There are a couple of diaries we've ended up with over the years that sit and collect dust. I had been meaning to throw them out, but they're sometimes the last things still around that belonged to someone now gone. I think there are a few other books that might be as old as the diary still on the shelves. I could see what I have that might also once have belonged to your family."

"It is a tempting offer, but I travel light," I say. "I plan to leave tonight for Buda, Pest, or whatever they're calling the area now that the two cities have been joined, and then on to Vienna."

"Ah, so you have what you came for."

"More than I expected." I look down at the letter and the diary. "Thank you."

He nods and doesn't say anything, and we regard each other. I cannot say what I should do right now with this leopard. He seems harmless, but he knows too much.

"It is best you go and we never speak again," I suggest. "You do not want to be caught up in my affairs."

"You can't control the hunger?" he asks.

I frown. "I control it fine," I grumble. "The fewer people who know about it the better."

His tail flicks as he thinks for a moment before he responds. "Of course. Well, glad I could be of use," he says and bobs his head. "Have a safe journey."

"Thank you," I say, and he lets himself out of the room, closing the door behind him, leaving me alone. I hope I don't regret letting him leave, because he could easily return with others.

I look back at the book and trace my paw pads across the worn leather cover. I should sleep, but now I want to read. I will need to have the innkeeper ship the book back to Vienna in my trunk, but before I do that, I want to know what Katarina thought. That need pushes out my fears of Ekrem revealing my secret to others.

I sit down by the candle, still wearing only a shirt, and begin to read.

∾

Hours later, I set the book down. I can almost hear Katarina's voice in my head as a distant echo. I had forgotten what it sounded like, but with her words, I can hear her again.

This volume dates to the years before the attack and a few years after. Most of it is about her marriage and the day-to-day parts of her life. Some of it sheds light on things I had forgotten, but it is nice to be reminded of them. Beyond the tragedies that struck our family, it seems she was reasonably happy with her life.

The pain of my death is recorded, and the surprise of the grave being disturbed is also noted. They seemed to have no idea what had happened, but the letter Katarina wrote suggests at some point she knew I was still out there. I skip around, trying to get a general feel of what happened. Father seems to have had bad luck in business, putting a strain on them. The last entry is from four years after my attack, and it gives me great pause.

It has been a tiring day, but I must record this lest I forget the details. Today, Gavrilo was fishing by the creek behind the house when he saw a bear on the opposite bank walking. He was dressed in an old-fashioned outfit, he says, and he had never seen the man before. He had a bow slung over his shoulder. When Gavrilo called out to him asking if he was lost, the bear turned toward him, and he saw a great raw scar ran from below his ear and across his neck. This specter, because no living person could survive a wound like that, floated across the creek, not touching the water, and then vanished suddenly when he got to the other shore.

Gavrilo is absolutely terrified, and it took me an hour to calm him down and get him to tell me what he saw. With the disappearance of Milovan, the butcher, a week ago, I feel something is going on in the village, and I will speak to the priest tomorrow, and see if he thinks these is a connection. Since Radic died, I have heard strange whisperings, and I have suspicions something unnatural is going on. I do not think this incident is just the overactive imagination of a young mind.

I will record what the priest says tomorrow in my new journal. I must now try and get some rest.

After that, there is a blank half page, and the other side is blank. There are no more pages in the journal either. Whatever happened is in Katarina's next journal, and who knows what happened to it.

Whatever it was, whatever happened, Katarina would have recorded it. She was a dedicated diarist, and if she filled this book up and planned to start a new one, she would have. Both she and our parents lived for years after this, although I don't know what happened to Gavrilo. There was no stone for my nephew.

I get up and pace, thinking. The apparition could be anything. Perhaps it is a child's overactive imagination or a spirit. Perhaps it is the ghost of the Huntsman, trapped in this world seeking revenge on the one who struck him down. The only person who might know where the next volume of Katarina's journal is is Ekrem. Even if he doesn't have it, maybe one of the other diaries he has might shed some light.

I sigh and halt my pacing, frowning. It will be dangerous to find the answers, but I need to know what happened. While I didn't plan to stay, leaving now will forever lock what happened away from me. The only person I can enlist in this endeavor is Ekrem. He knows Strasek, and it's even possible he might be able to point me to someone here who still remembers Katarina from their youth. That would be risky, but it might shed light on what happened that I can't get any other way.

Now, if I can trust him, that's another matter. He didn't seem shocked to find out about me, but I don't know how much he really knows about vampires. Not everyone believes in us, and I know I didn't. I also don't know if I have a choice in enlisting Ekrem's confidence now that he knows about my curse. If I don't, he could easily tell someone else, and that would complicate my search.

The reason for my curse and the secrets of the man who created me are here. I thought it was a fluke, but there's more to it. I never saw him again, but I did not seek him out. It's quite possible he never left this area. He could be somewhere nearby, carefully picking off prey in a large region to keep suspicions down.

All the secrets of my past are here in Strasek, but am I strong enough to seek them out? If my creator is still here, I hope so. I'll need to be strong to face him again.

The Seduction of Loneliness

I usually sleep like the dead when the sun is up, but the few hours I have before nightfall do nothing to relax me. Instead, it just makes me nervous, and I lie in the darkness all too aware I am a prisoner in this room. I am on my paws at dusk, ready to head out. There is just the faintest glow at the covered window, and after I light the candle to confirm the time, I cautiously pull back the cloth I draped over the window and open the shutters. On the horizon there is a little pink and orange, and from it I feel an unnatural warmth against my fur.

I miss sunsets. I can no longer look at a blue sky and see clouds or enjoy the golden hour as the sun rises or sets. I am forever trapped by any light more than twilight, and even then, I can feel the reflected rays of the sun on me, reminding me of what I can no longer see. Tonight, in the faded light, the village of Strasek looks peaceful and calm. It will not give me its secrets easily, but I will find them. I need to know.

First though, I must look presentable. I brush off the last of the graveyard dirt, careful to make sure it ends up on the sheet I've put down, before I dress. I decide to wear a fashionable waistcoat on top of my shirt, so I leave my shirt collar open to show off my neck ruff. I tuck my pocket watch in after connecting the chain to the waistcoat. Attired so I at least look respectable, I descend downstairs to the inn.

"Ah, Master Radic, sleeping in again, I see. You are quite the nocturnal animal," says Alina when she spots me. "I was going to freshen your room up, but I didn't want to disturb you."

I still have the blanket with the dirt spread on the bed. "That's not necessary right now."

"Nonsense, I wouldn't want you thinking I'm a bad hostess," says the badger.

"I would never think that," I say and then give her a warm smile. "I've left a bit of a mess pulling out my clothes. It wouldn't be fair having you go through that."

"It isn't anything I didn't see when I was married," she says, giving me wink and a smile. "I can handle it."

"Again, I wouldn't want to trouble you with that," I insist. "If you do wish to give me a hand though, perhaps you can pass me a few loaves of bread and a bottle of red wine. I have to visit the curiosity shop and impress on Ekrem for a favor."

She chuckles. "Ah, the business he came to see you for this morning continues. Let me get that for you then."

I give her a nod. "You are too kind."

Alina disappears into the kitchen, and I take stock of the crowd in the dining room. The Twisted Vine is a thrum of activity as people break bread together. This isn't like the restaurants of Vienna that are segregated by social class; everyone in the village eats here. Laborers and farmers wearing work shirts sit near merchants wearing elegant clothes. I see everything from simple dresses to tailored coats being worn by the patrons. Even the old lupine priest is taking his supper in the back by the stairs. Strasek is too small for the better off to socially isolate themselves completely from the poor. There is an uneasy companionship about that, but it's still there.

I turn and wipe the tear of blood from the corner of my eye with my paw. I just need to pretend a little longer I belong among them, and once I have the answers I need, I can leave them to their lives with my tainted self no longer darkening this place.

❧

When she handed me the basket, I could tell Alina had outdone herself just by how heavy it is. Inside are three loaves of bread, two bottles of wine, two links of cured sausage, and a large wedge of cheese. She's determined to see me fed and has given me enough food for a family. It's simple fare, but I'm sure it's all quite good. I wish I could eat some of this. I hope Ekrem is hungry.

Night has fallen, but the town is still alive for now. Even beyond the crowd in The Twisted Vine Tavern, I see some people are still out this Saturday night. The work for the week is done, and the villagers are enjoying themselves before church tomorrow. I am used to the paved roads of Vienna, but there is something about the dirt under my paws in Strasek that just feels right. Traditional life still thrives here, and oh how I miss its simple rhythms driven by the rising and setting of the sun.

The curiosity shop is a two-story structure, with light spilling out a front window. The second story appears to be where Ekrem lives and that gives me pause. If this is his home, I cannot just enter unless he bids me to. The innkeeper lives in the inn also, but I had written Alina previously inquiring about a room specifically and received a polite invitation in her response. I have not been invited here. I can feel the curse tugging at me, trying to slow my footsteps.

I walk to the front door, feeling how each footstep is heavier than the last. Instead of even trying to enter, I knock on the door.

There is silence.

I clear my throat even though I no longer breathe anymore and knock again, hoping no one notices me not entering an open business.

After a third knock, the door swings open. "I'm still open," says Ekrem before he notices me.

"I thought it polite," I offer, holding up the basket. "I would not wish to intrude."

"The lanterns are lit downstairs."

"Indeed. May I come in?" I ask hopefully.

He looks at the basket and then at me. "You can't enter unless I invite you in?"

It surprises me he knows this, but it's true. I clear my throat again, even though it's just a gesture at this point. Now is the moment of trust. Does he see me as a threat? "That's correct. Since this is your home, I am forbidden. Now if you would be so kind, I could use your help with finding out more about what I read in the journal."

There's a moment of hesitation before he swallows. "Come in and tell me what you need."

The resistance vanishes, and with a nod to the leopard, I enter the curiosity shop. Ekrem shuts the door behind me, but lingers by the door as I look around.

The store is stuffed with antiques, housewares, and other odds and ends. An oil painting of a lone house in the woods hangs against the wall above a table with fine china stacked neatly upon it. An armoire sits against a different wall with a woven rug leaning against it. On another table is a basket of old wooden toys next to some dusty books that appear to be primers almost as old as I am. Various lamps are scattered about. Nearly every square inch of this room is covered with things and trying to take it all in is overwhelming.

"You have quite the selection I see. Is there a place I can set the basket down?"

"In the back," says the leopard, finally leaving the safety of the door behind. "I'll show you."

I watch the tension in his tail as he walks past me. "I make you nervous"

He pauses and turns around to look at me—truly look at me, this time. He is wearing an ascot around his neck and touches it now with a bit of apprehension. "A bit. I've been thinking about this morning, and I realize I was perhaps rash in my enthusiasm."

There is a moment of silence, and I can hear his heart beating. He's within striking range, and I did not eat last night. The urge is always worse when I'm hungry.

"I know you've given up the safety of your house by inviting me in, but if I wanted to bite you, I would have done that this morning," I offer, pushing down that cursed desire to sink my fangs into his neck. "I trusted you this morning not to send someone for me, so now I'm asking you to trust me. You have nothing to fear from me."

He bobs his head in acknowledgment. Whether my words reassured him or not, I can't be sure. "I know, but I did not expect to see you again," he says, resuming his walk through the store into the back room.

"The diary you brought proved to be far more interesting than I thought it would be. It has given me more questions to ask than answers."

"What type of questions?"

I'm unsure how much I want to say right now. I don't know how much of the book Ekrem read either. "It covers only part of Katarina's life. I still do not know what happened to my sister's kit. There's at least one other volume to her diary."

"Ahh, I didn't realize it wasn't complete." He frowns, and his whiskers twitch.

"Would it be here?" I ask hopefully, as we enter the back of the store.

Ekrem chuckles. "Maybe."

I want to ask why he says maybe, but just walking into the back, I can see why. The shelves there are overflowing with goods. Old books, plates, tools, knives, all packed up in a disorganized chaos so dense that the light doesn't even reach the back. There's also the smell of old wood and dust—so much dust I think I've seen tombs cleaner.

The leopard gives me a sheepish grin. "I inherited the store a few years ago and have tried to bring some order to this mess, but it's hard. I occasionally find stuff I didn't realize I had in here, so it's possible the diary is somewhere I just haven't looked."

I look over the room. "Well, it's just one room."

"Oh, you haven't seen the basement. It's full of so much stuff that I can barely make heads or tails of it."

There's no place to even put the basket down except on his desk, which is perhaps the only place amongst the sea of mess that shows some organization. On it, an incomplete letter is sitting, the ink still fresh, still shimmering in the light of a small oil lamp. The only clear path in the room goes past it toward the stairs in the back. The only other part of the room free of wares is the space near the small stove for heating in winter.

"This is…"

"Chaotic, I know." He takes a deep breath. "Come, upstairs is better. I've managed to get the mess upstairs tamed."

"After you."

The leopard picks up a lantern and lights it before he leads me up a staircase, carefully holding his tail so as not to knock over any of the goods stacked on one side. Upstairs, though, things are much less cramped. The roof slopes in, but the two rooms are not as cluttered, and the apartment is lived in with only the general mess of life taking up space.

One room is a bedroom with a large four-poster bed. The door to the hallway is open, and sheets are scattered on the bed itself. The other is a living space with a hearth, a table, and a chaise next to a bookcase. Ekrem picks up a few old broadsheets off the table and gestures for me to put the food down there. "Sorry. It's not much, but it's home."

I set the food down and look around the space's rustic furniture. It feels quite plain, although I can see a few fancier items have made their way up here. There is a stove to provide warmth in the winter, a cabinet for dishes, and even more books—it feels homey. There's a window in the front and a dormer window on one side that must catch the light of day well.

He squeezes his paws. "I don't get much company outside of business, so you must excuse the mess."

"It's fine," I say. "If we can't find Katarina's other diary, perhaps there are some others just as old that contain what I seek."

"I'm sure, but do you have time to read all of those?"

"When you're like me, all you have is time."

"I thought you wanted to return to Vienna," he says, looking in the basket I brought.

I shrug. "I want closure. There's nothing really for me back in Vienna, but there's nothing for me anywhere, so I hang around the shadows and try not to get noticed."

"I know the feeling," he says, going to fetch dishes. He pulls out two plates from a cupboard before pausing. "You don't eat anything, do you?"

I shake my head. "No, but a glass for the wine would be nice."

He nods. "Despite that, you've got quite the haul in this basket."

"I know. Alina is too generous, and I don't know how to keep her from trying. If she keeps at this, she's going to draw attention to the fact I can't eat food. And the worst part is her cooking does indeed look wonderful."

"It's great. It's better than what I can do here, and after a long day, I prefer taking my meals there."

"Makes sense. The Twisted Vine is a very lively tavern, and I'm sure the company is good."

Ekrem returns with two glass goblets and a plate for himself. "It's decent. My uncle owned this store before me, and I don't think he was particularly well-liked. It's taken me a few years to get people to warm up to me." He sets down the dishes and opens one of the bottles to pour us some wine. "You aren't going to mind if I eat, are you?"

"No, no, go ahead and eat. It's something I miss, but I'm mostly over it. I need to get my own food later tonight."

He gives me a sheepish look as he pulls out some of the cured sausage and one of the loaves of bread. "Please at least join me at the table," he requests, and I feel compelled to sit as he prepares his meal. "Alina bakes really good bread."

"Indeed. Why do you take most of your meals alone though, if you eat there so often?"

"Ah, you noticed that."

"Both times I saw you eating, you were by yourself."

"That's just how it is. The village is small, and I'm a bit of an outsider. I didn't grow up here, but my folks aren't too far away."

"But you had family here?"

He takes a bite of sausage and chews before responding. "I did, and I visited Strasek as a cub quite a few times. No one paid much attention to me back then, and I tend to be busy with the store now. Leaves me feeling more 'around' than a part of the village. People know me, but I keep to myself."

"That's lonely for the living," I remark.

"Ha! Like you looked so much different than me sitting there brooding over wine two nights ago."

"Looks can be deceiving. I used to be quite the dashing fox."

"You still are," he says.

I can feel my ears getting hot. "Well, not like I was."

"What do you mean?"

"I was adventurous, playful, alive … now I'm just here."

I feel a handpaw on my own. "I'm sorry for what happened to you."

Has anyone ever felt sorry for me since the change? I know my parents and sister did, apparently, but I was too stupid to seek them out. Too afraid. I cough in what is a truly living motion. "It's been hard, but if you help me, I can find closure to this cursed journey."

"Of course."

His handpaw is still on mine, warm, unlike my own. I go to pull it back, but he holds on, wrapping his digits around my own. "You don't have to be so compassionate for me. I've done things," I say. There are things I try not to remember, and they're all just below the surface. Things I can't let out again.

"Would you do them again?" he asks cautiously. He was relaxing around me, but now I can see his guard has gone back up. My ears must have betrayed my concerns.

"God, no. I couldn't control it then. I was just hungry. The hunter in the shadows. Those days have haunted me for a long time."

He searches my features. "What changed things for you?"

I take a deep breath. "I was up to my old hunting tricks, and I met people while stalking a meal who thought I was just an eccentric bohemian. This was before the term had been coined, but it's the best I have to describe how they saw me. There were too many of them to take them on, so I let them carry me along that night as their newfound friend. They were drunk, their guard down, but in that moment, I was still alive. I was just a scruffy looking fox who made a decent drinking partner. That night made me remember, and it stayed my fangs. I realized then how much of life I was missing out on. I decided that night to drink of life's goodness, not of its blood. Vienna has always been home to music, and I enjoyed some of the great symphonies there conducted by those who wrote them. Unfortunately, age comes for people; when you don't age, you have to go elsewhere after a point, or they'll notice. I returned to Vienna ten years ago after spending fifteen years away. Previously I was gone for thirty years."

"So, you do admit it's isolating," he says before he sips some of the wine with his free paw.

"It is, but you see things you can't with a shorter life. I've watched how things have progressed and the birth and dissolution of empires. I remember when the emperor issued the Serfdom Patent, giving the serfs their first rights. I saw the long march toward freedom that entailed for the peasantry. It gives you perspective."

"I hadn't thought about that. Has a lot changed in the last hundred years?"

"Yes and no. Some things are quite obvious, while others are subtle. Then there are the things that don't change, which is what is sometimes surprising." I flick my fingers. "On a simple note to that effect, you can let go now."

His ears flick back and he pulls away, taking away the warmth of his touch. "Sorry."

"It's okay. It's just the most physical contact I've had in … well, since I stopped feeding on sapient life."

"That is a harsh way to think of it, but do you not live?" he asks me earnestly.

I'm taken aback by that. I know I'm dead, even if I can pretend I'm still alive. "What living can I do?"

He gets up and walks over to me. "Whatever living you want."

I study the leopard leaning against the table, his lithe frame. I can read his body language well. I cannot say I am not intrigued, but the suggestion catches me off guard. "What you suggest is what got me in trouble a hundred years ago."

"You're the one who told me to get naked. Plus, I saw you parading around your room in the inn."

I place a handpaw on my chest and give him a coy smile. Maybe there is still some life in me. "You caught me indisposed."

"Perhaps, but I know a man like you when I see one. You made no effort to dress beyond pulling on a shirt."

Indeed, I had not. He got me there. I hadn't even considered it when I knew he posed no threat to me. "Perhaps that was a bit forward of me."

He quirks an eyebrow.

"Well, it was. Just because I've lived over a hundred years doesn't mean I'm good with company anymore. You forget things."

"Clothing is an odd thing to forget," he says coyly.

I enjoy being teased and teasing back, but I have to ask this directly. "Is an interest in men what sets you apart from the others in the village?"

He chuckles. "It is one of the things, yes. Strasek is still a small town."

"Oh, I remember. People get in your business when they shouldn't, but that doesn't stop one from pursuing their desires."

"Indeed. But it is you who I should ask to forgive me, if I am too forward. You have other concerns."

"If that's what you want..." I pause to consider for a moment, "then get naked."

He blinks at me, and he slowly reaches down to undo one of the buttons on his vest. "And if I do?"

That's a good question. It sounds fun, but what is desire to me anymore? What can I hope for in this world when all I can do is take from it and corrupt the people I know?

"I don't know," I say softly.

He reaches up to run a paw through my cheek fluff. "You do not love anymore?"

"What is there to love?"

He searches my face, looking at me carefully. "Life itself. How could you let yourself survive for a hundred years and refuse to actually live?"

My ears fall. "I know the answer to that question, and yet I don't know the answer to that question. I am—" I falter, unsure what to say about myself. "I am confused as to what counts as living anymore," I say finally. His head tilts, and I take one of his paws, bringing it up to my chest. "My heart is still now. My body is cold. It is only the curse itself that animates me."

"And are you just a curse and nothing more?" Ekrem asks me.

My ears are pinned back, and in that moment, I see myself and my years in the darkness behind me, and the leopard in front of me. My resolve solidifies then. "No." My free paw clenches. "I can be more."

He smiles then, warmly, and I can almost feel the sun on his golden fur with the warmth of it. "Good."

"So, to repeat my earlier command, take your clothes off, please, and I'll show you how I can be more."

"No," he says. "Take yours off and show me you won't bite first."

I flick my tail and make a big show of considering before I stand up and start to slowly undress, first removing my coat and then my vest, meticulously undoing each button to see how he reacts. When I am down to just my shirt and trousers, I pause to let him say something.

"Go on," he says.

I nod and undo the buttons of my shirt and let it drop before undoing my belt and taking off my trousers. Once again, I am in the fur, and the call of the night makes my fur tingle. It is nothing to slip into my bat form now, but that's not what's exciting me now. "Well, I have nothing left to hide now."

"Au contraire, your sheath still hides the real jewel."

"Present me with something worthy of it showing, and you'll know the entire length intimately." I lick my fangs.

He undoes his vest and pulls off the ascot around his neck. The fur there is matted from the fabric, and I can see where I would need to bite to end this leopard, but what I'm going to stick him with isn't my fangs.

"Better," I whisper, feeling a stirring I have not felt in a long, long time as his trousers fall away. He is quite handsome, after all, though I had not allowed myself to appreciate it fully until now.

"Let me help,' he says, getting down on his knees and burying his face in my crotch. He pauses when he realizes my body really no longer has the warmth of a living being, and I expect this to be over then as he glances up at me.

"I'm sorry," I say, trying to pull away from him, but he grips me, and I can feel his claws dig into my side.

"No," he says. Then there is a raspy tongue on my tip, and in that exact moment, I am doomed to be under his spell. Any power I might have held over him is gone, and this is his moment to play me. There is warm breath again in places I never thought of it being, and I feel myself gasp as I harden—with a need once again found.

I quiver as he gently touches my shaft and takes it into his muzzle. I swear I can feel the sun upon me, not burning but warm, like a pleasant summer day. Is it the spotted gold fur of the leopard or the intoxicating effect of arousal? I'm not sure, but I cannot stop myself from thrusting into the eager muzzle between my legs.

In my ears, I can hear his heart beating, the way he gasps around my shaft, and for a moment, I am just a fox with regular needs. My hunger is for Ekrem himself, and I can feel myself heading toward climax too fast.

When he breaks off and heads to the bedroom, I follow, entranced. Ekrem gets onto the bed, and he presents himself to me on all fours, ready and willing. My shaft is wet already, and since he offers no oil to make my entry easier, I take him as I am. He is tight around me and warm, while I am ice piercing him. Yet, in this coupling, I can feel a building heat as I find a slow rhythm and take him with my weight on his back.

Instinctively, my fangs want to lengthen so I can sink then into his neck, but I push down that urge. I lower my muzzle to his neck; he tenses, but I only nibble gently and playfully as I thrust into him. I always loved it when someone did this to me, and the way he bucks under me tells me he enjoys it also. In my haze of lust, he is my sun, and I the moon, only able to shine my light indirectly in the night.

Too soon, though, I feel him shiver under me, and he clenches down upon me. My knot has swollen, and I get a few more strokes going before I too climax, and he slowly collapses under me. We are tied together.

"I may have gotten carried away," he pants. "We should use lubricant next time."

I bark amused. "Sometimes, the moment just happens. Here, let me hold you," I offer.

"Sure," he says, and carefully I roll to the side. He remains tied to me, but my weight isn't upon him. Together we lie there, spooning, and I absorb the scents of the leopard, the house, and the tangy spice of lovemaking. His breath is sharp next to me, and I listen to his pants.

"That was intense," he says.

"I know," I say, muzzle buried into the ruff of his neck. I can still somehow taste the sun on his golden fur, and yet it does not burn. "Thank you."

"For what?"

"Something you cannot understand. It was … it means a lot to me what we just did."

His muzzle tilts up so he can try and catch a glance at me even though I'm behind him. "You're a strange man."

I chuckle. "As I said, time had given me a different perspective with so many years behind me."

"It sounds educating. You can accomplish things others cannot ever achieve in a single lifetime."

My ears flick back. "Yes, but there's a lot of doing nothing."

He's silent for a moment, thinking about something I can't know. "Well, if you'll help me, we'll see if I can find the other journal. There's still places I haven't looked yet for it."

I smile. "I've got the time if you do." I can feel I have softened a little, but we're still tied. "When we're done here, of course."

"It would be my pleasure."

~

The store's back room is indeed a maze. It requires unpacking and repacking in order to sift through the merchandise. Thankfully, Ekrem has a good idea where everything is, so it doesn't take long for us to start locating old books. The basement will be a larger endeavor when we start on it.

Three hours in, though, we've found nothing of note, and our clothes are covered in dust. The few promising diaries we encounter don't seem to mention anything of use after a cursory glance. I'll have to read them all to be sure, but even for someone with years on their side, it's irritating.

Especially when the book I'm actually looking for has to be somewhere.

"Are there any others?" I ask, picking up another book from a shelf in the back. It's well past midnight, and I have forgotten how many of these I've already skimmed.

"Not really. These things don't sell, so I sit on them."

Glancing in the book, the name inside is at least familiar to me. "This one could be promising."

Ekrem is digging through a stack of leather-bound volumes stored in a wooden chest. "Then give it a look."

I nod and walk over to his writing desk. "Mind if I sit?"

He glances up, whiskers dusty. "Be my guest. I moved everything to the side earlier."

I sit down and push to the side the other couple of books of interest we found earlier. By doing this, I accidently disturb his stack of business correspondence. When I do, I see the person he was writing to earlier, Lorelei, the vampire hunter.

I freeze for a moment and then glance toward Ekrem. He's still digging in the chest. I carefully pull out the letter and read it until I get to the point he mentions me. The ink is fresh, and it says everything I feared about the leopard.

"So you knew…"

He glances up at me. "I knew … oh fuck." He sees me holding the letter.

I get up. "This is a trap, isn't it?"

"No."

I glance at the letter and read. "He's arrived in town as you expected."

Ekrem stands up. "It's not that."

I walk over to where he is. "That's not what this letter says."

He swallows but stands firm. "You're not like she told me you would be."

I get close to him and place my handpaw against the bookshelf to trap Ekrem there. "Listen to me and listen to me good. You live right now because I want you to live. Just because I can control my hunger doesn't mean I have to do it."

He swallows, but stands firm. "You can't do it. I already can see it's not in you. Maybe it was, but it's not in you anymore."

"You think I'm a coward? I can feel the life inside of you," I say, closing my eyes. "It calls to me. I can feel it. I need only to sink my fangs into you, and I could drink you dry, all of you. You would be far sweeter than the wine we drank earlier."

He is silent, his breathing shallow. I can hear his blood in my ears, and the hunger gnaws at me since I did not feed last night. "I need only to give you a drop of my own essence after draining you to bind you to me as my thrall," I whisper.

"Is that what he did to you?"

I open my eyes and study the leopard's face. Since the moment he met me, he's known who I am. His eyes are as big as saucers, and yet he does not seem frozen in fear. "He used the power to raise me, but he didn't claim me. I do not know why. Maybe he didn't understand what he was doing. I only learned years later how that works."

"You raised someone yourself?" he asks, with just a slight quiver in his voice.

"No. I met others like me. It was enlightening, but we have different ideas of what being a vampire entails. Now, what did Lorelei tell you?"

He looks at me, his whiskers twitch a little, but his eyes narrow. "That I was to tell her what you came here for."

I growl. "So tonight was your way of keeping me busy?"

"No. I made my own opinions," he says.

"Did you now?" I growl, getting close. My hackles are up, and my fangs slip out naturally.

He can see the change, but he stands his ground. "It's in the letter. If you wish to use my words against me, use them all."

I look down at the letter in my other handpaw.

"At the end," he whispers. "I was writing it when you arrived."

I glance at the last paragraph and read. "I watched his movements as you asked, and he told me he was going to Bucharest in the morning. I know—"

There's nothing after that.

"I could tell you meant me no harm," he says.

I let my arms fall. "Why did you plan to lie to Lorelei?"

"She told me you were evil and could not be trusted, but there's nothing about you that's evil. I can see that."

I look down at my black paws. "I hate what I've become, but there is nothing I can do to change it. All I can do is control it."

"Then let me help you. Is there no cure for this?"

I look up at him and search his face, trying to read what he's thinking. Surprisingly, he seems honest, but that collides with my own fears of being discovered. "Why do you trust me?" I finally ask him.

"Because I've seen real evil, and it's not you. I have felt the corruption."

I frown in confusion. "What did you see?"

He looks me in the eye and swallows. "I can't be sure, but it may be the one who turned you."

A False Dawn

If I had a heart that still beat, it would have skipped. My mind races at the implication of what Ekrem just said. The one who turned me is still alive? That can't be. "Tell me everything you saw," I whisper.

The leopard gestures toward the stairs. "You look shaken. Perhaps we should go upstairs to sit down. There is the other bottle of wine," he suggests.

My ears are down, and I realize I have tucked my tail defensively, going from aggressive to scared almost instantly. "I thought he was gone."

"I don't know for sure whether it is him, but is the one who turned you a mustelid of some kind?" Ekrem asks me.

In my mind, I can see a flash of his smile, as he leaned forward to whisper honeyed words that dulled my senses and ensorcelled me. If he told me his name, I do not remember it, but I will always remember the feeling of warmth he brought to my cheeks and the horror he cursed me with. "He was a stoat. I saw the black tip on his tail."

Ekrem considers. "I thought I saw a weasel, but in the dark, it can be hard to tell."

"But you saw another vampire?"

He nods. "Yes, come, let's open the other bottle of wine, and I'll tell you what happened."

I nod dully and follow Ekrem upstairs and through the house, my mind racing. If the one who turned me is not gone, what does that mean for me? What happens if I kill the one that made me? If this is a different vampire, is he perhaps tied to what happened when I was turned?

Back in his room, I sit down at the table. Ekrem pulls the other bottle of wine out and opens it. Carefully he pours some into a goblet and hands it to me.

I take the offered drink and look down at the dark red liquid, feeling myself falling into its depths. "This information could save me."

"Save you?" the leopard asks me, pausing as he fills his own glass.

I gently swirl the glass of red wine, contemplating it. "If you saw the one who made me, I can find and kill him. I will have appeased my curse then."

"Does it work that way?"

"I don't know. It might free me from the eternal night, or it might not. Even if it doesn't, he is too dangerous to let survive."

Ekrem nods.

"So tell me what you saw," I ask, looking up from the wine glass.

The leopard picks up his wine and takes a sip. "First some background. Before I owned this store, it was my uncle's. Uncle Ismail was always eccentric, and trying to work out the way he organized this place has convinced me he had a different way of thinking. Ismail always could quickly find things in here. I have spent years trying to reorganize this place and the extra stock, and I still find things I didn't know were here.

"Before he died, my uncle used to travel to Huszt, where my parents live, to sell excess goods. He employed an assistant back then who would watch the store. Ismail came to visit shortly after I turned eighteen, and he insisted on taking me out to celebrate."

"And?" I ask.

"We went to the tavern, and we drank. He had me good and going. I was feeling no pain when it came time to stumble home. The night was dark, the moon was not out, and we went up the street drunk, turned a corner and what I saw will never leave me."

Ekrem takes a deep breath to steady himself. "There was a weasel with his face in the neck of a wolf. I thought he was a man showing affection to another man at first. That itself was strange to see in public, but as I watched I realized that wasn't what was happening. They weren't kissing, or anything else similar for that matter. Instead, he had his fangs in the neck of the wolf, and blood was running down from the wound. We must have disturbed his meal, for he did not wish to leave. I could see the hunger in his eyes, yet I could feel myself being drawn toward him. I knew not who or what he was, but I suddenly wanted to approach him even as I could see what he would do to me."

I no longer felt the chill of winter in my body, but a frosty cold going down my back that felt like my spine had been replaced with ice. "That sounds like him," I say softly.

Ekrem nods and continues. "In that moment I was helpless in a way I have never been before. Maybe the weasel didn't notice my uncle Ismail, or he was able to resist the pull of the weasel. Uncle threw up the lantern he was carrying and charged the vampire. That seems to have saved our lives because he fled before my uncle, leaving us with the dying wolf. We tried to save him, but he was too far gone.

"When you came into the tavern and you told me you wanted to speak to the priest, I knew you did not wish to kill anyone. You sought only the solace of the dead, not the blood of the living. That is how I knew you were not evil. I had seen the weasel and the wolf in the tavern before the attack, which made the whole thing much worse. They seemed happy, but the wolf must have been under the weasel's spell. For this, he paid with his life."

I drum my fingers on the table. "That's what he did to me. He ensnared me in a moment of weakness, and he compelled me to join him for what I thought would be a tryst. Instead, I became what I am." I pause to consider. "Are you sure it was a weasel though and not a stoat?"

"I think so, but it was dark."

"If it wasn't him, it's another vampire. On that, did the wolf rise?"

"We told the local priest, and he took matters into his own paws to keep him from coming back."

"Good. A vampire made out of hate like that only turns to anger."

Ekrem considers. "Are there other ways to make one?"

"I have heard rumor of those created due to love, so the vampire would not lose that person, but it is only a story. The few others of my kind I've met have not been the most talkative, and I have not been in the mood to talk either."

"Are there many of you?"

I shake my head. "No. Most vampires are solitary, but there are those that stick together. I found there was safety and solace in isolation. Too many vampires attract the hunters, and it is easier to stay in the shadows when you're alone."

He nods. "So will you seek him out?"

"It will be dangerous, but yes." I ball my paws into fists. "If he's the one who created me, I cannot let him live."

The leopard's ears go up. "Is that wise?"

I bark out a laugh. "No, but I've been running for a long, long time. I came here for closure. I will tie off this loose end, even if it costs me my own life."

"And what about Lorelei?"

"If she gets to the other vampire first, by all means, let her take care of him, but she is looking for me. Maybe there's someplace nearby I could stay."

"What about here? Would the basement work?"

It would, but do I trust him? It would be easy for Lorelei to find me that way, but he seems honest. The only caves I know close to Strasek are quite shallow and offer little protection and safety. There is a deep cave I used on my way to town, but it's quite a distance from here. "Is it dark down there?"

"Very."

I swirl the wine in my goblet around. "Let me make arrangements tomorrow night with Alina, after I figure out how to handle my trunk."

"I can pick it up for you to send it on and say I'm making a trip out of town," Ekrem offers.

"That would work. I'd like to do some more looking tonight to see if there's anything else in the journals we do have. There could be something else we missed since I was focusing on looking back to when Katarina was alive."

He picks up his goblet of wine. "Hopefully we can find something."

❧

Unfortunately, the search is unfruitful. I go back over the diaries I've already looked at. Skimming them too quickly means I'll miss something. Skimming them slowly takes time, and as a result, I come upon nothing throughout the night. I do find quite a few interesting anecdotes about brewing in one of the diaries, but I'm not planning to make my own beer.

After a while, Ekrem cannot hide his exhaustion, and I bid him adieu a few hours before dawn. He mumbles a goodbye and plods off to get some sleep before the store opens. I leave the basket with the remaining food with him and set off to find my own meal while I still have time.

My mind is racing as I stroll through the village, thinking of the possibilities about what happened. Is he still here? Can I find him? Do I even have the strength to take him on? Yet, the night is still, oblivious to my inner turmoil. I see no candles or lamps lit, but that does not mean someone is not awake, waiting and watching. I don't know what happened or where this mysterious bear specter came from, but there is one thing I do know—I'm famished.

Taking one of the roads out of the village, I quickly find myself wandering down a rutted lane out in the fields that surround Strasek. I make sure I get over a hill where anyone who watched me leave town will not see me. Finding a haystack, I take a moment to pause in the shadows near it, looking around. Satisfied that the area is deserted, I take my clothes off and fold them up, tucking them under some hay. Then I step out into the moonlight and slip into my bat form.

I beat my wings, feeling the joy and freedom it gives me. I would love to fly circles around the fields like I did last night, chasing the shafts of moonlight the clouds make, but business has to be handled. Flapping harder, I push up and away from my former home. The nearest village is a few miles away, but I don't need to go that far for my meal. I just need to find some cattle a discrete distance from any nearby farmhouses.

I search for half an hour, and I'm rewarded with a remote field by a copse of pines that is down the hill from a farmhouse. I circle low to the ground before I let my form slip and land softly on my footpaws, naked and kneeling against the ground. I take a moment to listen to the wind and the insects in the field before I get up. The cattle are sleeping and it's easy to creep up on one and whisper the words that makes the cow only kick a leg as I reach down and sink my fangs into her neck.

The blood is warm and coppery, and I am so hungry. Yet even though I know it will keep me going, it's missing what makes it delightful. Cattle do not have the intelligence of someone like myself, and the blood is flat in my mouth. It lacks the fullness of a sapient creature, but in my hungry state I could drink my fill and be satisfied.

Too soon I have to break off before I kill this poor beast. I smooth the fur down before I move to the next cow and repeat the process. After that, I'm still hungry, so I take some from a third, and that finally sates my thirst. I take only a little from each, and I keep my bites clean and precise. They might be a little sluggish in the morning, but the farmer should be none the wiser for it. It would not be prudent to raise his suspicion that something is amiss. My fang marks are small, and the puncture wounds should heal quickly in a day or two.

When I am done, I walk to the copse of pines, letting the night and its magic tickle my fur before I slip back into my bat form, and I take flight. The wind carries me a little further away from Strasek, but I must make for the village. Already in the east I spot the lightening of the sky that heralds the coming of dawn, and with it my mortal enemy, the sun. I need to be back to my room and the safety it provides. Although I do not age, I still need to rest. I can feel a growing weariness in my body from the lack of rest and the full meal, and it will be nice to sleep a full night today.

ȣ

The sun is close to rising when I finally return to the inn. Already there is a warmth against my fur from the sky. I had not planned to be gone for so long, so I didn't leave the window to my room open to attempt to climb up to it. The inn is dark, and while I could possibly find a way in as a bat, I would have to abandon my clothes I retrieved from the haystack. I first attempt the latch on the front door before I get creative, which I find is unlocked. I bless my luck that Strasek is still too small to require people to lock their doors at night apparently, and I enter carefully, pausing to listen.

My ears swivel back and forth. I'm already working on an excuse for early morning entry, but I don't hear anything. I wonder if perhaps Alina is up already baking bread for the day, but the fire in the hearth has gone out. No light comes from the kitchen.

Not wanting to disturb her or arouse suspicion, I carefully cross the common room, but at the stairs I pause. Something is wrong. There's a sweet smell in the air, and I can feel my fur prickle in excitement before I realize what it means.

I smell blood.

Even though I just ate, the momentary rush comes to me first before the concern for whose blood this might be sets in. I sniff again, and realize the scent is strong, yet also stale. This isn't just a drop from a splinter or pricked finger.

With trepidation, I try to climb the stairs silently. They creak a little as I ascend and I pause, but all is silent. There is just a little light coming in from outside when I reach the top of the staircase, and in the shadows, I see Alina. She's lying in the middle of the hallway, and there is no call to my senses from her life essence. She is dead, with a pool of dried blood near her.

Shaking, I carefully walk over to her. I feel both the exhilaration in myself at the scent of blood and the horror that Alina is dead. It can't be too recent since the blood has dried. The badger is still wearing the clothing she had on last night, and she's lying on her side. Her neck is exposed and bloodied. I kneel down next to it to confirm my fear. Against the matted fur I can see two fang marks next to each other.

I touch my own neck, feeling the two healed gashes there under my fur. This is not a precise bite like I make, but the bite of someone who doesn't care. This is the bite of someone who wants you to know how someone died and who wants to draw attention to their crime.

I sit back on my haunches, squeezing my handpaws so that I can feel the claws dig into my pads. "I'm sorry," I whisper.

My words sound hollow, and I realize I shouldn't have come. She deserved better than this. I need to go. Whoever did this did this for a reason, and the further I get from Strasek, the safer the people here will be.

Except I know that's not true. No, no one will be safe if I leave because no one here can fight someone like me. To leave them to this fate is a coward's path. I left this village defenseless and alone before, but I didn't know what I know now. I know who and what I have become. Whoever did this did this to get me to leave, because they know I know their weaknesses. They don't think I will seek out the truth of what they've done.

"I will make sure whoever killed you pays for this," I say to Alina's corpse, clenching my fists. "You deserved better, and I will not rest until they are slain."

I get up, and that's when I see the bloody pawprints, leading toward my room. The door has been left ajar.

Carefully, I walk over and push the door open. The window is also open, and there is a bloody spot on the windowsill. For a brief moment I have to wonder if I did this. Have I suddenly lost control of myself and entered some type of fugue state? What if I wasn't with Ekrem most of the night?

I'm shaking, and I have to steady myself against the door frame. Even inside there is a growing warmth on my body.

Dawn is coming, but I need to know. Hesitantly, I look down at my paws.

The black fur is clean.

I want to take a deep breath, but I can't. I didn't do this, but who did?

I look closer at the pawprints. The toes are positioned differently than my own, and while I am not a tracker, there is no fox print.

I look out the window, and I can see the sky is lightening. The sun will rise in a few minutes, trapping me here in the inn. There will be no escape from paying for this crime, if I stay.

"Well played," I snarl as I spring into action. Quickly I grab Katarina's journal and flee the room and thunder down the stairs and across the common room. I'm not sure if there are other guests tonight, but they used my room for their escape intentionally. At the front door I pause and pull it open quietly, trying not to look too guilty. Stepping out, I can hear voices in the distance.

Hurriedly, I walk across the street, and I can feel burning pain on my head from the sky. I grit my teeth as I pass a wolf who turns, curious at my suddenly hustling by. I pull my collar up and keep walking, the book clutched under an arm.

I could fly away, but to where? There's nowhere close I know to hide. Maybe someone has a basement I can break into and take my chances in.

Entering the town square, Ekrem's shop sits quietly, and I practically sprint toward it, seizing upon it as my only option.

I reach it and try the door, but it's locked. Frantically I start banging on the wood. "Ekrem," I call out. People are going to notice me, but I don't have a choice. "Ekrem!" I yell, pounding on the door.

Over the distant horizon the sun breaks, and even in the shade among the buildings, I know my time is up. My body becomes pain, and my fur screams.

"Ekrem, please," I cry, slamming into the door, feeling myself starting to go. There's burning, something is cooking … oh god, I'm cooking!

"Ekrem," I whisper, slumping against the door as motes of dust envelop me. This is it. This is the end. At least the morning light is beautiful as it kills me.

There is a click from the lock and the door opens. I fall into the store and the dim interior. I don't feel the floor when I hit it.

Eternal Dusk

I awake in darkness with some type of heavy canvas over me. I'm on a wooden floor and there is nothing but pain left in my body, endless hunger, the smell of burnt fur, and a voice in the distance.

Wait, two voices, I think, but I only hear muffled sounds. I attempt to lift my head so I can hear what they're saying, but it hurts so badly I fall back to the floor.

There is nothing after that for a while.

Later I feel my head being lifted up. The canvas is no longer over my face. "Drink this," someone says, as a cup is pressed up against my muzzle. Haltingly I lap at whatever is in the cup. It's salty and coppery, and I think it's blood, but I can't tell. I can't really taste anymore. The sensation is dull and muted against the pain.

When I'm done, my head is lowered down and I doze off again. I dream of Katarina holding Gavrilo, shortly after he was born. She's clutching the young kit closely to her chest as tears streak her fur. I see my parents again as they tell me they want me to take over the family business when I'm old enough. I walk the road I died on with the one who killed me, and when he turns to sink his fangs into my neck, I bolt upright and scream.

"No!" I yell, and the dream dissipates.

I'm still covered by this piece of canvas, so I scramble to pull the cloth down off my face. The bite in my neck itches fiercely, and I reach up to touch it and rub the spot. I blink trying to see where I am, but it's dark. Through an open door, I can see into Ekrem's store and the sliver of moonlight on the floor there. I am off to the side, among stacks of merchandise in the back room.

I hear the sound of scrambling. Then a thumping sound of paws on the stairs and a light blinds me, as Ekrem comes down them, carrying a lantern.

This light doesn't burn though, but just makes me blink, trying to focus.

"You're awake!" he says, surprised.

"Yes." I pause, trying to figure out what happened. "Alina, she's dead."

"I know," he says.

"She was bitten—"

"I know. We took care of it."

"She could still rise," I say, trying to get up, and wince. "Ow … this hurts."

"We took care of that also."

I tilt my head. "How long have I been out for?"

"A little over three weeks."

"Weeks!" I say in surprise, ears standing up.

"You've been awake a few times when I've fed you, but you've just been lying there. I couldn't get you upstairs or down into the basement, so I had to leave you here."

I pull the canvas off my body. I am lying completely naked with some dirt scattered underneath me. "What happened to my clothing?"

"I had to throw that out. It was covered in this weird dust of burnt fur, and it smelled like a tomb. Lorelei would have noticed."

"She's here?" I ask.

"She was," he says, ears going back. "She had me help with making sure Alina stayed dead. The attacks have created quite a stir."

I try and process this. "There were others?"

"A farmer went missing two weeks ago. No idea what happened to him and no sign of him has turned up at all. One of the school children says he was ambushed last week by someone, but they managed to escape by running to a neighbor's house. Other people say they have seen things at night, but it's hard to say what is real and what is people's paranoia."

"How, how did you know it wasn't me?" I ask softly.

He smiles. "I didn't at first, but why would you come to me vulnerable like that if you thought I would turn you in? Later, I heard the tracks they found weren't those of a fox. The consensus in village is they belonged to a weasel and that weasel also got you. Lorelei thought you might be working with the weasel."

I nod. "Well, I most certainly am not. Can you help me up?"

"Sure," he says, putting the lantern down and coming to help me get up. I feel stiff and it takes me a moment to get my balance once I'm on my footpaws. I turn around to look myself over. My fur is short, like I just blew my coat. I can only tell where my fur burned off and the sun reached skin because those areas feel tender still. My tail is thin like I've been sick.

Ekrem notices me looking myself over. "I can barely tell you were hurt," he says. "Once I started feeding you, the fur started to grow back in."

"I heal quickly, but I have never been burned like this before." I rub the fur along my arm where it was exposed in the morning light. Everything feels fine, but I still have a terrific headache.

"You looked rough," Ekrem said. "I got the dirt since I thought you'd need it."

"It does help me rest," I say, as I look over my right handpaw, flexing the digits. I remember it burning, the fur coming off in the dawn. Now, the fur is neat and clean. It's healed surprisingly well. "It's like it didn't happen, yet I can still feel the kiss of the sun." I take a sniff at myself and wince. There is the unmistakable scent of burnt fur still clinging to me. "I see why you threw out my clothing."

"I tried to clean you up, but you need a bath."

Gingerly, I brush the dirt off my fur. I still feel a little unsteady. "I need to procure some clothing first. I don't know what happened to my trunk."

"Oh, I have it. I ended up with the trunk to see if I could sell it after Lorelei looked it over." The leopard points, and next to some dishes is the steamer trunk I had sent to The Twisted Vine. "Some of your taste in clothing is rather old fashioned."

I clear my throat. "I look very striking in a ruffled shirt when I'm not covered in bits of dirt, thank you. I was quite the fop in my youth. It's not my fault the world moved on." I go over and run my paw over the trunk. "Striking, youthful, full of life—it's probably what got me in trouble to begin with. I had far too much rakish pride back then." I open the trunk and start digging into it. I see he's placed Katarina's diary inside. Everything appears to still be here, although it's been shifted around.

The leopard chuckles. "You still have your looks."

Carefully I reach into the corner and feel around until I find a small purse tucked in to a hidden pocket stitched into the trunk's liner. "Oh good, I am not destitute," I say, hefting the purse. I close the lid of the steamer trunk, turn around, and sit down on it. "Looks can be deceiving. See beyond the fur." I flick my tail into my lap to make myself decent.

"I see a naked fox sitting on a box."

"Sitting on top of most of what he owns in the world. I have some money in an account in Vienna, this purse of guldens, and that's it. There's no castle. There's no romantic, tragic love story in my past. There's a fling that I never consummated, and darkness."

Ekrem doesn't say anything but just looks at me. I watch the way the light from the lantern plays across his face. Finally, he speaks. "I see someone who still thinks they're a fop."

I smile. "Perhaps, but what else?"

"Besides the dirt and lack of clothes, you look rather normal."

"Looks are not everything," I say. "Nor is eternity. The great stoic philosophers knew that all we have is the present." I consider for a moment and look down at my paws, frowning. My ears go down. "And yet here I am worrying about what was instead of what is."

"Because the present is shaped by the past, and the future will be shaped by the present and the past."

"Indeed." I close my eyes and shake myself to right my thinking. "You said something about a bath?" I say, opening them. I should focus on the now.

"Yes. I could draw some water from the town well, but it's quite late. Dawn is only a few hours away."

"A bucket and a cloth would be okay for the moment. I can get the water myself."

"Lorelei is still looking for you. I had to keep her out of the back room, so she didn't notice the smell. There's only so much potpourri I can leave out."

My ears go back. "You didn't think to tell her I was in the other room?"

"I thought about it. I thought really hard if I was harboring a murderer, but as I said before, your eyes are not the eyes of a killer. There's sadness in them. There was sadness in them when I first met you at the inn, trying to carefully make your way to the stairs, and there was sadness in them when you thought I might have ratted you out to Lorelei the night Alina died." He walks over to me and puts a digit under my muzzle to tilt it up gently so I can look at him. "I don't think these are the eyes of a killer."

My dead heart aches. He's given me more forgiveness than I have ever given myself. "You say that so easily, yet I know I have done things that I have tried hard to atone for."

"I think we all have things we regret, but I admit, my regrets are much more mundane." He seems to want to say something else, but he drops his paw and shakes his head. "Do you want the water still?"

"If you'd be so kind then, and I won't trouble the rest of your night. I can sleep in the basement today while you work. It should be dark enough down there."

࿐

When Ekrem said the basement was full of various odds and ends, he wasn't lying. Even though he said he's been working on sorting it, stacks of goods and crates filled to the brim are still everywhere. The scents down here are of dust and stagnation, with hints of decay from the damp that seeps in through the dirt floor. After I wash up, I have him leave me here with a lantern to get some sleep while I ponder.

Down here, I won't need to get any graveyard dirt to help me rest, but I'm not tired either. Now that I've awakened from three weeks of cold dead sleep, my mind is racing with everything that has transpired. I need to figure out what's going on, but I don't know where to look. Lorelei is looking for me, and whoever killed Alina wanted me gone, but there's something else. Is the Huntsman still alive? Is that the specter Gavrilo saw? Also, how did Lorelei find me? I don't think she can track me when I fly, so she would need to know I was coming to Strasek. How did she know that?

It's possible Alina tipped her off, but that would require Lorelei to have known her. If she didn't, that means she knows about my connection to the village. The only records that I know of that would mention it are locked away in the village church, and in Katarina's diary.

It's quite possible she has the other volume of the diary. With that, she'd know where to find me, and what happened. I only know of her from a vampire I knew named Riccardo who had heard of this fox who was hunting our kind. He thought himself a connoisseur of the ladies and was going to dispatch her. I found him despicable, but Lorelei somehow found him easy prey and took him out. A few weeks after Riccardo disappeared, I saw her, in an alley near an opera I used to frequent. She was almost a shadow in the night, but the iron tipped crossbolt gave her away. She called my name, and with that I knew she had me marked. I fled and kept low for six months. I've still not been back to that opera house.

I get back on my feet and start pacing. Could Ekrem still be working with her? That's possible, but he had his chance to kill me. His concern for me seems genuine. Either he didn't tell Lorelei I was still alive, or she needs me alive for some reason. There's no way she'd show mercy to me, but what she wants, I don't know. She's persistent, but for her to follow me for four years? That seems extreme.

If she's this persistent, I doubt she's left Strasek. It's also possible she came here because she wants to settle other business. Whatever happened to the Huntsman, if she has the other diary, she has all the clues to know what happened.

With Alina dead, though, the inn is likely closed. Just like I need a place to stay, she needs the same. Ekrem didn't say she asked him to stay with him. Also, unless she's told all the villagers why she's here, she's not just going to be walking around town with a crossbow looking suspicious. It's likely she has a place to stay nearby, and if she does, she could have the journal with her, assuming she's ever had the journal.

I think back to the alleyway, and her calling out my name. I stop pacing and my fists tighten. She didn't just call me Radic, she called me Radic Horban.

I stopped using my surname after the change. I didn't want to bring shame to my family. She certainly knows my story from somewhere if she knows that name. I can almost guarantee she has seen the journal or it's in her possession. As for where she is, that's something Ekrem will know.

⤙

Just before dawn, Ekrem comes down to check on me, and I tell him I will be okay. I want to ask him about Lorelei, but I resolve to wait till tonight. I tell him to go about his day as he normally would and leave me here. All I can do right now is wait and rest. Still, rest does not come. Perhaps it is because I slept too long. The basement also isn't completely dark. A tiny sliver of light filters in from a small crack in the foundation that Ekrem probably doesn't realize is even there. It's too diffuse to hurt me, but the thought of any sunlight makes me anxious.

It and the little light that creeps past the basement door at least gives me something to work with. I should have asked Ekrem for matches so I could relight the lantern, but I had thought I'd sleep. Instead, my day is restless, and fitful, and the hours pass uneventfully. I doze only a little and listen to the footsteps above me as Ekrem moves about the store, accompanied by the creak of the floorboards. Sometimes people come inside, and I hear voices, but I can't make out what they say. I feel the itch in my body to do something, to get out there and find the answers I seek, but there is nothing

I can do. There is just the quiet silence of this damp, makeshift tomb, and my unbreathing, lifeless body.

Eventually the light from the crack fades, and I can tell the sun's tyranny over me is slowly vanishing as it slips down in the sky. At dusk, the door to the basement opens, and Ekrem comes downstairs, carrying a lit lantern.

"Radic?" he calls out. "Are you awake?"

I had given up trying to sleep a few hours ago and have taken to alternating between pacing very slowly in the little clear space I can find down here and pretending I'm a statue made of stone that details a fox. Carefully I turn my head toward him, while perched on a chair like a gargoyle.

"Yes…." I hiss. I'm sure my eyes glow in the darkness, picking up the light from the lantern.

The leopard looks at me from the bottom of the stairs, his tail lashing. He tilts his head. "What are you doing?"

"Amusing myself," I say, getting off the chair. "This is the only piece of furniture I could dig out silently, and it's too dark to see what other relics of the past you've got lurking under the tarps in the corners."

"You wanted it dark, didn't you?" he asks.

"Yes, but I see no better in the dark undead than I did alive. I just can't be in sunlight. I didn't really sleep, but tomorrow I should sleep better."

He nods. "Did you want to look for the next journal tonight? I've taken some time the last few weeks to go through stuff, but it's not turned up. It's possible I missed it."

I shake my head. "I don't think it's here. Where is Lorelei? I must find her."

He's taken back by that. "Why on earth would you want to see her?"

"She knows things I need to know."

He tilts his head, looking at me in confusion. "You want to talk to the woman who wants to kill you?"

"Talk is the wrong word. First, tell me how you met Lorelei."

He thinks as he heads back upstairs, beckoning me to follow. "She came here a few months ago and told me she was looking for a fox who only went out at night. She told me you called yourself Radic, and that you were dangerous if approached. She asked me to send a telegram to her in Vienna if I saw you, which I had to go to Herzok to send. The instructions I got back were to record your actions and send her a detailed letter, but to also make a copy of it. She planned to come to Strasek, if she could quickly arrange travel."

"When did she tell you I was a vampire?" I ask as I follow.

"That was obvious when she said you only went out at night. After the incident that occurred with Uncle Ismail, I understood why she was approaching me and the need for secrecy."

"So, no one else knew besides you and Alina I was coming to Strasek?" I ask Ekrem, as we climb up to the second story of his store.

He shakes his head.

"Are you sure no one else at all knew?" I say. "It seems strange Lorelei knew I would come here before I did."

"If Lorelei told anyone else, she didn't tell me. She did say she spoke to my uncle three or four years ago and made the same request."

"Interesting," I say, pondering. "She knows far more about me than I know about her."

"She does indeed seem to know your history, but she doesn't know you, I noticed." We've reached the living quarters, and he sits down after motioning to the other chair. "You're quite the charming fox. She mentioned nothing about your personality at all."

I chuckle as I sit with him and lean forward. "So, what are you supposed to do about this charming fox now, if you did see him again?"

He gives me a sly smirk. "Just let her know. I should send another telegram to her in Vienna."

"Does that mean she's returned to Vienna?"

"Not as far as I know, but she didn't actually tell me where to find her if I did. She told me the office in Herzok wouldn't know where else to send them."

"So, she left no forwarding address."

The leopard shakes his head.

"And she isn't staying at the inn?"

"Doubtful. Alina had a brother who has come to town, but he's still working on sorting out what to do with it. I think one of Alina's adult children might take it over, but they're in Budapest. The burgomaster is putting pressure on the family to reopen, but she understands it's still a time of grieving."

I wonder. It couldn't be that Lorelei is like me, could it? "Does she come only at night to see you?"

Ekrem shakes his head. "No, she came during the day, but she certainly is cautious. She doesn't want to be found."

"Indeed, but she can't be too far away. She's got to be somewhere around here."

"That assumes she's still looking for you, of course."

I flick my tail. "She's a vampire hunter, and there's a vampire loose in the area. Two, it seems. If she's been looking for me for four years, I don't see her backing down suddenly when her quarry is nearby. She has the advantage of having both the day and the night at her disposal in this chase. What did you tell her about me when she came by after Alina died?"

"I told her we had talked, but I didn't tell her about the journal," says Ekrem.

"That's fine, but she knows who I am from somewhere, and the only reliable source that covers who I am is going to be Katarina's other journal." I consider. "Do any of the other towns have telegraph offices besides Herzok?"

"Not yet. They've got one because that's where they plan to build the station when the railroad reaches us."

"As I recall, Herzok is a three-to-four-hour walk. I can fly there faster, but it's still quite a ways."

"Wait, you fly!" he exclaims in shock.

I smile sheepishly. "Just as a bat. It's the only good thing I've gotten from this curse."

"Yes, but you still fly," he insists, eyes lighting up.

"Trust me, I would give that up in an instant to feel the sun warm and nurturing against my fur and to know the taste of food."

He shakes his head. "There are those who would trade that away to know eternity."

"And what good is eternity when all it brings you is pain?"

"Am I pain to you?"

I hesitate. "No, you are a warm glow." I take his handpaws in mine. "And one that does not try and burn me away. You are everything I am not, and for that, I am thankful."

He blushes.

"But I must find Lorelei and see if my suspicions are right. The journey to Herzok should be quick, and if she has the journal, I'll..."

He waits. "Well?" he asks me.

"Somehow get it out of her possession. Unfortunately, I'd have to walk back with the book."

"Well, it's only four hours if you walk slow," he remarks.

"I'm sure I can do it in under two if she's chasing me, but it will be worth it. I need answers."

The leopard nods, and I smile, trying to reassure him. What I don't tell him is that I'm willing to pay with my life if

I can find these answers. It's been a long hundred years. It's time to settle all this.

The Lonely Hunt

I ask Ekrem if he can leave a window open for me upstairs, and he offers the one in his bedroom. It is there where I make the change to my other form. One moment I am standing there, a naked fox in his prime, and the next I am small and free. He gasps at the sight of the bat that has taken my place, but I am already beating my wings to launch myself out of the window. I circle the house once and catch sight of Ekrem watching me before I climb higher and away, letting the night embrace me. Catching my bearings, I circle above the village to find the road to Herzok, and then follow the line of dirt through the fields and into the distant woods.

The flight only takes about half an hour to complete and reminds me how fast I am when I take to the air. The only travelers I see out are a farmer with two oxen pulling a wagon heading for Strasek and a stagecoach, bouncing down the road quickly toward Herzok. I shadow the coach for a few minutes out of curiosity. The driver, a bear, seems none the wiser to my presence. I stay out of the light of the lanterns hanging from the stagecoach, and he doesn't notice me at all. However, I can tell the horses are slightly unsettled by my presence, so I push ahead. The rest of the road is quiet and deserted.

Once it enters the woods, following it is a little trickier, so I drop down to skim below the branches for a while before I again climb above the trees, feeling the freedom of the night sky. After the forest, I emerge on the outskirts of Herzok, but unlike Strasek, I can see that Herzok has changed. Progress has come to this corner of the empire. A hundred years ago, this village was no different from Strasek, but since then it has tripled in size and become a proper town. Church steeples reach for the sky and smoke from fireplaces make the air above the town thick. On the edge of town, I can see a mill with a smokestack, and nearby a straight, slightly curved path leads into the nearby woods. A railroad line has already been surveyed, and some work on it is underway. It is just waiting to be linked with the rest of the empire.

I'm surprised by the town's growth, but it is good that progress is occurring here. Without the railroad, the people here will be left behind. However, this growth also brings a whole other problem for me. If Lorelei is here, she won't be easy to find. Scouring the streets from the air, I count four different inns, each with their own common rooms, and a half dozen taverns. This is a town big enough to hide in, but not one so big I will go unremarked upon if I somehow draw attention to myself.

First though, before I can investigate, I need to find some clothes to wear. I circle around the town, looking for someone who has left their laundry out overnight, hoping to find something that fits me. The first house I spot with laundry left outside has only dresses, so I pass by it. After flying on for twenty more minutes and having to double back, I spot a farmhouse with promising looking clothes. I fly low to the ground and when I get close, I change back to my true form, landing in a crouch.

I stay there, and swivel my ears, listening for any sounds. If someone saw me, I will need to flee immediately. I couldn't possibly make up an excuse about my sudden appearance that would satisfy an astute observer. After a minute of only hearing insects, I feel satisfied I was unnoticed. Only then do I go to inspect the clothes.

Even though they're freshly washed, they have a bit of wolf scent about them, which is probably the owner's. There are two dresses and some woman's underclothes which I ignore, but there's also a pair of men's trousers, multiple shirts, and even underclothes. The shirt I select is a bit big on me and a little worn, but it covers me. It's still a little damp, but it will have to do. There's also a vest, which I take. That, thankfully, is dry, but it presses the damp spots of the shirt against my fur. I opt to spare the owner the indignity of me borrowing his underwear. As for the trousers, they are a little loose and long on me. I roll the cuffs up, but they still want to slip off.

Carefully going to look in the nearby barn yields rope and a knife to cut it with to size a belt for myself. With the vest being big on me, I'm able to cover that up a bit and look at least decent. The lack of footwear would be an issue in Vienna, but out here, many still go barepawed. I even find a stash of gulden in the barn, tucked into a glass jar, while looking for a knife. I don't want to do it, but I take two coins in case I need some money.

After I'm dressed, I glance at the farmhouse. Lantern light glows in its windows and woodsmoke slowly curls out of the chimney. The lupine farmer and his wife seem none the wiser to my presence, so I slink away toward a nearby country lane and follow that into the settlement. I want to stroll through town and see if I can get a clue on where Lorelei might be. Unfortunately, unless I run into her directly, it won't be easy to find her.

Walking through Herzok reminds me of Vienna, but on a much smaller scale. It has streetlights and the roads are paved, but the buildings are much more modest here. Still, a lot has changed since my youth, and I see many modern buildings have been built. Unlike Strasek, I recognize nothing about this place. The Herzok I'd known was a small sleepy village I had little reason to visit. This Herzok is one full of life and people. Houses with light from lanterns inside line the road interspersed with shuttered stores and an occasional business open at night. The village I visited a century ago had almost no one out after dark. That's not true anymore. I see many people are out and about, and while I am quite used to cities, I try to look unremarkable so nobody takes an interest in me.

The central square, with its warm glow of lights, would be at home in a quiet corner of Vienna or even Paris. Few of the old timber houses are left in the town's center. Instead, they've been replaced with brick buildings that crowd next to each other. The older structures that do remain in town sport fresh coats of paint.

The tracks have not been laid on the new railroad alignment yet, but already a train station is nearing completion to link this area to the rest of the empire. It is also here, in a small wooden building, that I find the telegram office Ekrem spoke of. It sits open, with a gas lamp outside. I pause for a moment, considering. If Lorelei's here and looking to communicate with anyone outside of the area, she'll need to come here, but who knows when she'll come or how often. I turn around, looking at the nearby streets.

They're quiet, but down one I see a tavern. Walking toward it, I realize it's more than just a tavern but a full-service inn with a common room. Above the door hangs a sign with the words The Lupine Prince written above a well-dressed wolf holding up a tankard. I consider for a moment and a fox exits the tavern and politely holds the door open for me. The resistance to my entrance is now gone, so I go in to seek out a table.

The tavern is somewhat busy, and I approach the bar, where a wolf tends to the drinks. "Fancy a room and a drink, friend?" he asks me when I'm close enough.

"Just a drink," I say. "Also, can I grab a table?"

"Sure, sure. What can I get you?"

"A bottle of red wine."

He nods and picks up a glass. "Any preference on the vintage?"

"Just something dark."

"Coming up. Grab a table and I'll be over."

I select a table by a window to watch the street and sit down. A minute later, the wolf brings over the bottle and a glass, which he sets in front of me. I pay the man the guldens I took for the bottle and sit back to think as I open it.

This seems to be the closest place to the telegram office I can stay for an extended period of time without lurking outside, but that doesn't mean she's here. Right now, I'm taking shots in the dark, but I can't just go around asking for Lorelei, can I? Then again, what happened in Strasek can't be a complete secret. Maybe I can get the bartender talking.

I pour some wine, and make a show of drinking alone, while I wait for the crowd to thin out some. About thirty minutes later, the bottle is half gone, and I'm feeling heavy and laden in my stomach from the wine, but now is my chance. I get up and go over to the innkeeper and set it down on the bar as I take a stool.

"If you've got a minute my good friend, I've got a few questions for you."

"Hmm?" he asks, looking up at me.

"Yes. I'll be traveling to Strasek tomorrow, and I was wondering what you could tell me about it."

"Strasek, why would you want to go to that accursed place?" says the innkeeper.

"Accursed, what do you mean by accursed?"

"Well," he takes a moment to set down the glass he's been polishing. "There are bad things afoot there. That place, it used to have strange happenings long ago, but we all thought those days were long over. A few weeks ago, things started happening there again that make me think the corruption never left. Now, we've got strange things happening in Tarcsa and all over the region. People have died in mysterious ways or just disappeared completely. There's also this woman looking for people, and I don't trust her. She was here a few days ago asking questions you just don't ask people."

I am taken back. Perhaps this will be easier than I thought it would be. "What do you mean by questions you just don't ask?"

The bartender chuckles. "The type of questions you don't go around asking people, about like what they eat and when they sleep. It's very curious. My advice to you is don't go to Strasek, if you can avoid it, and if you've got business there, get your business handled and get out. There's something bad going on over there. Anyway, there isn't a place to stay there right now."

"My good friend, I would like to know what exactly I'm walking into, because my business unfortunately is in Strasek."

The innkeeper looks me over and frowns. He leans forward across the bar. "I can't say if it's the villagers or not, but something ain't right about that place," he whispers. "There's someone stalking the village at night, so don't be caught there after dark. Whoever it is, they're not the type of person you want to run into."

"That sounds like a myth," I offer, seeing if I can get more out of him.

"You'd think that, but this has happened before, about a hundred years ago or so. Some people went missing under mysterious circumstances and turned up with bite marks in their necks. The whole region was up in arms back then, but then things stopped. I wouldn't give much credence to anything like that, but the innkeeper at the only inn in Strasek turned up dead recently with those same bite marks. Since then, others have vanished or turned up dead. Apparently two people went missing in Tarcsa a few days ago. They did find them eventually, but I hear what they found wasn't pretty."

"This sounds dangerous indeed."

"It is, but that's not the strangest part of it."

I cock my ears. "It gets even more curious?"

"Oh yeah, but you best not worry about that. Just avoid the woman."

"How will I know who she is?"

He chuckles. "Oh, you'll know. She's got this way about her, and she's working for some noble too. Not sure who, but it could be the emperor himself for all I know. She's one of the strangest wolves I've ever met though, and trust me, I've got some family that you would not like."

My ears go up. "Is that so?" This isn't Lorelei, so who is the wolf?

"Oh yeah. Now, enough chatter. I can see you worrying about things you shouldn't. Just handle your business by day and avoid the wolf if you do see her. And whatever you do, don't make a deal with her. She is asking for things that people shouldn't, and if you ask me, I think she has the power to collect, but not without her noble friend present."

"What could she ask for that people shouldn't ask for?'

The lupine innkeeper gives himself a shake. "A prick of your finger to get your blood like some type of mad scientist."

"Blood?" I say softly as my mind races. One drop of my blood is all it takes to turn someone. Is someone trying to become a vampire?

"Yeah," he says. "The whole thing is curious, and I want no part of it. It's best you keep away from her. I don't know anyone who did give it to her, so don't worry about it though."

I'm unsure what to make of this turn of events. I want to ask more, but I don't want to arouse suspicions. "I'll do my best. Thank you, friend."

"No problem. It's my job to keep people happy and safe," says the wolf with a little wag in his tail.

I let him get back to his chores as I sit at the bar pondering what he told me. Who is this wolf he spoke of? Things don't fit together, and until I get to the bottom of this all, I'm going to be in the dark.

∾

After leaving the tavern, I wander around Herzok for a bit, trying to quell my stomach. It tolerates red wine, but not well. I also just drank a whole bottle of it. This bit with the wolf also just makes me uneasy, so I stroll around town for over an hour to help ease the ache. I'd walk around more, but it's getting late, and I don't want to draw attention to myself by wandering around after most people have gone to bed. I head back to where I got the clothes from, and I leave the clothing under the clothesline in the grass, after rubbing them into the earth a bit. I want to force the owners to rewash them, and I need to cover my scent with something. Hopefully they think a wild animal got into them or the wind knocked them down. To keep up the appearance, I also pull down one of the dresses and make sure it's also dirty.

The length of rope I used as a belt I take with me and walk naked across the fields, picking at one of the ends with a claw to unravel it. I eventually drop it into the mud at the bottom of an irrigation ditch after making it badly frayed. Then I let the change take me and feel the earth fall away.

Once I get some height, I begin circling Herzok, getting a better feel of how it has evolved. As far as I know, none of the other nearby towns have railway stations planned for them, yet the line looks like it will pass through Herzok to somewhere else.

Trying to follow the line out of Herzok, however, I find that it ends on the outskirts of town. Perhaps they haven't surveyed further, or perhaps this might be the end of the line. Abandoning that wild speculation, I decide to head for Tarcsa to see how that looks. It's the next place to investigate, and while it might be too late to wander the town, I can at least get a look at it.

I set out in the general direction, but I quickly end up over woods, unsure of where it is. I have to turn around and fly back to Herzok, and then find the road to Strasek before I can set out for Tarcsa. Following that, I know roughly when to turn to the east. Picking up a stream that flows through the fields, I catch where it intercepts the road from Strasek, and turn to follow that toward Tarcsa, passing the little hamlet of Hez. That at least doesn't look like it's changed much, but that's because it's still just a small cluster of houses.

I can see the old castle in Tarcsa on the horizon when in the distance I hear a screech. I glance around, trying to locate the sound, and something slams into me, knocking me to my side. Quickly, I try and beat my wings to steady myself and change directions. Out of the corner of my eye, I see another bat. It screeches again and attempts to dive at me.

I twist away from it, beating my wings, trying to get some distance. I've never had a bat attack me like this before. Getting another glance at my assailant, as I make the tightest turns I can, I see its wings are broad, and its face fanged, just like mine is.

This isn't a normal bat. It's a vampire in bat form.

I dive then, trying to gain speed, and I can hear whoever is pursuing me trying to keep up. I've never even thought what fighting in this form would entail, so I'm having to learn quickly.

They have apparently attempted something like this before, because I feel fangs try and rake my back as they've caught up with me, and I'm forced to turn to the right and then bank quickly to the left, trying to cause them to overshoot.

From the cry I hear, I think this helps, but I don't think I can outrun them. Diving down, I'm almost to ground level when I let go of the form, and tumble back into my true self, rolling across a field of grain. I climb to my feet shaken, bleeding, and naked. I'm cut up from the attack, but in my normal form, I might stand a chance.

"Show yourself!" I call out, hissing angrily.

The bat veers around me, and circles me shrieking, waiting to see what I'm going to do. There's nothing I can use as a weapon here, but as it circles me, I count the seconds, and when I think I have my timing right, I lunge at the bat, trying to swat it out of the sky with my handpaw.

My claws are dull, but my reflexes are sharp. I manage to connect and knock the creature to the side, raking it in the process. I turn to pounce, but my quarry screams bloody murder and escapes my grasp, flying up, favoring a wing. I wonder if they're coming back, but they fly off, leaving me in the field of grain alone.

I sigh, and flop down onto the ground. My back has gashes from being bitten in the air, and I'm sore from hitting the ground. I debate walking back to Strasek, but that would take a while. With a grunt I get up and check the skies. My attacker seems to have decided to flee, but it doesn't hurt to be cautious. Satisfied they seem to be gone, I change back into my winged form and head toward Strasek.

❧

On the way back I ponder what I've learned tonight. Is the vampire behind these attacks? Why is this wolf asking people for their blood? None of this makes sense. I make a stop near Hez to feed on some cattle, but I'm cautious and only take what I need. Back in the air, I wonder if I'm being tailed.

Ten minutes later, when I arrive back in Strasek, I decide to swoop in low to the buildings, flying between the houses toward the square. No one is out to notice me. Arriving in the central square, I find a house with the upper floor overarching the first a little, and I land upside down, hanging off the woodwork to wait.

The town is quiet, and I do not hear the beating of wings or any type of pursuit. After twenty minutes, satisfied that I've escaped my pursuer and they've not followed me back here, I head toward the curiosity shop across the street and quickly enter the open window.

Changing back to my fox form, I make a soft thump as my paws land. Ekrem rouses himself from the bed.

"Did you find her?" he mumbles, glancing up at me, while I am still bathed in the moonlight.

"No," I say, walking back to the window and closing it. "But I found someone else."

He tilts his head and gets up off the bed, and wrinkles his nose at me, sorting out the scents I've brought back. "Who?"

"Another vampire, whoever they are." I turn around. "You can see they did not take kindly to my presence."

He frowns and turns up the lantern that has been sitting by his bed. "You're hurt, and bleeding," he says, surprised, looking over my naked body.

"They found me in bat form. I hope I gave them as bad as they gave me, but they were in Tarcsa."

"Tarcsa?" he asks. "I thought you went to Herzok."

"I did. I learned in a tavern something happened in Tarcsa recently, so I thought I'd go look at the town. This vampire, whoever they are, is apparently there, or was at least."

He considers. "I haven't heard anything."

"The bartender I talked to didn't know all the details. There's also someone else in this who seems to be investigating what's going on, a wolf of some kind. The bartender didn't say much about her except to tell me to avoid her."

Ekrem frowns. "Why? What's going on?"

"That's a good question," I say, sighing. "I don't see how this all relates, or why it is happening now."

"Is Strasek in danger?" he asks, grabbing a cloth to tend to my wounds.

"It shouldn't be, but that's what I need to determine. I'll be fine also, after I let this heal," I say, noticing the concerned look he's giving me.

He pushes me to turn me around. "I did not spend three weeks watching you to have you go get yourself hurt again."

"I'll be fine!" I protest.

"Let me get some bandages, and I'll bind these up."

I sigh and grumble. "I am not so fragile I cannot face fate as it comes. The road before me is not easy or sunny."

"That doesn't mean I want you broken."

Me, broken? Hardly. I will see this though. I should protest, but the stern look on his face and the lashing of his tail dissuades me. Instead, I just sit down and let him go get some bandages.

The Moon's Touch

I awake at dusk, rolling over with bandages wrapped around my chest. There's a heavy blanket over me, and I push it aside. The tyranny of the day is over, and I am free to again search for answers, but the bed is comfortable. I could rest here for a bit. The bed smells of Ekrem and that's nice.

Wait, why am I on a bed? Where is the dirt?

I sit up suddenly. I am in Ekrem's bedroom. Besides just the blanket, the window has been covered to protect me. I feel around the bed sheets for dirt, but there isn't any. I slept on the bed without any dirt at all.

I give myself a shake. I've slept without dirt before, but without the comfort of the grave, my rest is always uneasy and unsettled. I remember Ekrem binding my wounds, but I did not mean to sleep when he told me to lie down. Apparently, I did, and my night was restful. That surprises me.

I ponder if something about myself has changed, but nothing comes to me that would alter my curse. A few minutes later, there's a knock. "Are you awake?"

"Yes," I say, and Ekrem enters, carrying a bowl.

"I thought you might be hungry, and I went to the butcher shop this morning before I opened the store to get some food for you. I asked the butcher to save me some blood so I could make blood sausage tonight. I picked up my order about half an hour ago."

My ears go up. "You didn't have to do that."

"I know, but you were hurt, and I thought you'd appreciate it."

"I do," I say. He hands me the bowl and I lift it to lap some of it up. It's already cooled, but it's still got enough of what I need.

"I hope it's okay."

"It is. Thank you." I go back to drinking it, careful not to make a mess on his bed. When I'm done, I hand the bowl back to Ekrem and get up. Carefully I pull back the bandages to see how well I've healed. My wounds have closed, and the fur has filled in a little already. It would have taken weeks for mortal me to heal wounds like this.

"That looks a lot better," he remarks.

I stretch, feeling how my muscles protest. "Yes, but I am not indestructible. Feeding does help me heal faster."

I see Ekrem shift his weight subtly and his tail curl up a little at that comment, and it's a reminder of the monster I've become. Now though isn't the time to dwell on that.

"There are bigger concerns than my condition, but I'm also at a loss what to do."

"On that, I did hear about what happened in Tarcsa today from a customer. There was an attack three nights ago, but this woman was there. She seems to have intervened and saved them, but she insisted they be brought to the castle afterward."

"Lorelei?"

"No, someone else. I don't know what her name is, but she stopped the vampire. There's also something weird about her."

My ears perk. "Weird how?"

He frowns. "She apparently has all these charms braided into her fur. She's asking people about their blood, they say."

"It's the wolf the bartender told me about, isn't it?"

"Probably. My customer said our mystery wolf is asking for something particularly strange. Sanis vital?"

"Sanis?" I consider for a moment, pacing. My Latin is poor, but something clicks. "Sanguis?" I ask Ekrem.

"Ah, that's it. Yes, Sanguis. There was another word too that begins with a V."

I frown and walk over to the window. "Sanguis means blood in Latin." I turn toward him. "Sanguis vitae?"

"I think so," he says.

I'm silent, considering. "What is sanguis vitae?" Ekrem asks me when I don't respond.

"The blood of life. It's a nickname for vampire's blood."

"Why would someone want that?"

I look at my black furred paws. "Drinking it grants you eternal life. You live forevermore, free from sickness in the shadow of night. To seek that out … that's brave."

"It seems strange she stopped the attack then."

"Indeed, that is curious, but you can't just acquire the blood of a vampire easily. If one bites you, they can gain power over you, but I've heard if you can extract blood from a vampire, you can purify the blood of their corruption, it is said, and gain that power for yourself. However, the myth that vampires can't cross running water simply isn't true, so who knows if that's true or not."

"How do you purify blood?"

I shrug. "No earthly idea. I just heard many years ago from another vampire that this was possible."

"That sounds like some type of dark alchemy, but I can see why someone would seek that out."

"Eternal night is not as fun as mortals think it is."

"Perhaps not, but to have nothing but time? There are those who would desire that greatly. Especially those who feel time is against them."

I snort and shake my head, turning to look out the window over the darkened village. "The intense loneliness of it gets old."

"What if someone takes the person they love with them into that eternal night?"

That does catch me off guard. I leave the window and walk over to him, taking hold of one of his handpaws. He looks at me, confused. "While it's a sweet thought, why should two lovers suffer the same fate? Your fur and body are warm, and I crave that. Your heart beats with life I can only dream about now. To take someone willingly into that night is to rip everything warm about them away. The sun still kisses your fur, and I can feel the faint echoes of daylight upon you."

"You can feel the sun upon me as I can feel the cool moonlight upon you?" he asks.

My ears go back and I feel suddenly self-conscious. "Yes … and you feel moonlight on me?"

He is close to me, and I can feel the whiskers on his muzzle brush mine. "That or the call of the night. There's something about you that's different when I touch you."

"I don't breathe anymore, and my heart doesn't beat."

"Yes, but there is a subtle energy in your fur that's just different."

My ears suddenly feel hot. "Huh. I've never known that."

"I do not claim to understand what you have seen or been through, but I will help you find the truths you seek."

"Thank you," I say and lean forward to touch muzzles. "I appreciate it."

His heart beats faster. "You're welcome," he says and then breaks off the embrace. "So, what's next?"

"Good question," I say, considering. "I do have a question, though—what happened to the castle in Tarcsa? Does it still stand intact, or is it a ruin now? I did not get a good look at it."

"It still stands, testament to the Dragomirka family. I am told they generally prefer to reside in Buda with the royal court, but they use the fortress as a summer retreat."

"Then their archives likely remain there."

"Indeed. They offer access to their vast collection of books to the locals of the nearby villages." Ekrem tilts his head, thinking. "Do you think the journal is there?"

"No, but I bet this is why the wolf went there. There's something I'm missing. Perhaps I will have better luck tonight, but I suspect they have something of interest in their library."

"I can go in the morning, you know. I have business I need to conduct in Tarcsa at some point, and I can stop by the archive and see what they might have."

"I wouldn't put you at risk."

"What risk is there when the sun is up?" he asks me.

I go to open my mouth and pause. "Good point. I am just anxious to find out what is happening."

"For a man with eternity at his fingertips, you are certainly in a hurry."

I shrug. "I'm making up for lost time."

"Impatience is dangerous, even for you."

My ears flick. "It is, but—"

He lifts a paw to wag a digit at me. "Surely you can wait a day or two. Whoever is out there might be looking for you, tonight."

"Probably."

"Let me take you somewhere nice, tonight, where they won't be."

I tilt my head, caught off guard by this. "What do you have in mind?"

"Someplace you might remember. You know the millpond up by the old grist mill?"

"I do. It's still there?" I ask.

Ekrem scratches the back of his head. "It is. One more question. When was the last time you went swimming?"

&

The pond is located a ways out of town, and I go with Ekrem as he takes the trail to get there. We decided going in my normal form would be risky, so I cling inside of his coat as a bat, so as not to draw any attention to myself. If anyone is watching the store, they won't notice me. Over Ekrem's shoulder there is a bag containing my clothes.

Wrapped in his coat, I can feel the warmth of his body all around me. I can hear his heartbeat clearly, steady and strong. My tiny claws dig into his shirt, so I don't get thrown around, but that also makes him reach down to adjust my positioning a few times. There's also something safe about being enveloped this way. It's so reassuring that when we're outside of town and Ekrem opens his coat, I feel a touch of sadness as the warmth is taken away.

As planned, I drop down to the ground and change back to my normal form. The leopard hands me the bag.

"You were like a bit of ice inside my coat," he says, as I pull out a shirt for myself.

"You were like a warm, enveloping blanket that felt like it was just beyond my reach," I respond.

His ears flick and he looks away. "That must feel quite odd."

I shrug. "I'm used to it. A hundred years of lifelessness and you get used to it. You stop attempting to breathe, you stop attempting to be what you're not."

I'm sliding on my trousers when he speaks up. "Do you ever want to just risk seeing the sun, just to feel warm in that moment before it's too much for you?"

I pause, one footpaw on the ground and the other in my trousers. "All the time, but you saw what happened to me when dawn came." I pull my trousers up all the way. "I don't understand why I can't see the sun either."

"What do you mean?"

I shrug, ears back. "I am cursed. My body is corrupted by the bite, but why does the bite do this? I have no idea. Is it magic? Is it science or some disease? I don't know. Perhaps it is an affront to God himself, and he casts me out of the light, but there are no answers as to why. I just am."

Ekrem reaches out toward me. "Before you start, you're not evil."

I catch his handpaw. "Ekrem, you have been kind to me, and I greatly appreciate that, but feel the ice in my touch. I am corrupted by this. No matter what you might think of me, you must remember that … I cannot be anything but this. All I have is the night. I can never have the day."

"Yes, your touch is cold and I can feel the lifelessness in your fur, but even now, as you hold my paw, I can feel it warm, if only just a little."

And indeed, as I hold his paw, there is a bit of sun that exudes from his fur. Not the hot burning of daylight, but the slight hint of life and warmth. Even in the icy embrace of death, I can feel his life, not just for the promise of blood it brings, but that there is more to it. Something else.

"I … I feel it too," I whisper.

"Then perhaps you aren't cursed to wander forever. Perhaps there is more you could be?"

"A cure?" I shake my head. "It can't exist."

"Are you sure?"

My ears fall. "No, but I've never heard of one. The only cure anyone has ever offered to me is the stake."

"Well, it doesn't hurt to look, does it?"

That catches me off guard. It wouldn't hurt, and in a hundred years, I never even thought of looking for one. I have just existed. "I confess, I have never considered there could be a cure."

"When I go to Tarcsa, I will see if there is anything in the library that could help you."

"Thank you," I say, and we set out upon the path. I had considered if I should go all the way to the pond with him in his coat, but he wanted to just get me out of town discreetly. With how Ekrem talks energetically about his day, I don't think he would have been happy with me just wrapped in his coat. It also would not have looked good if someone saw him talking to himself. As for myself, with the murder of Alina, I do not wish to show my muzzle around Strasek.

Lucky for us, the path is deserted, and the moon is full and bright. The dirt of the earth feels warm against my paws, and in a fit of foolishness, I can imagine myself dropping down onto the path and just rolling in the grass to capture that fleeting warmth of day.

The path passes through trees and past a field before it climbs up to the gristmill, built just below the millpond. The weir and mill were already old when I was young, but it still is in use. We walk past the mill up to the pond, and follow the path around to the back, out of sight of the mill. The sandy little beach I remember is still there.

"I used to go swimming here when I was a kit," I remark.

"Oh, I think children still come up here," says Ekrem. "I'm sure we won't be the first to swim in the dark either."

"The water will be cold. Are you going to be okay?" I ask.

He gives me a smile. "I'll be okay. My fur is thick," he says, unbuttoning his shirt.

In my youth, I likely would have said no to this, because I know the water will be chilly. The millpond was always cool, even in summer, but I barely feel the cold anymore. Still, after I've undressed and stepped into the water, my footpaws certainly register the difference. It doesn't feel chilly to me, but I can tell it is.

Ekrem's fur stands up along his tail and hackles once he gets into the water. "It's brisk," he offers, wading into the pond.

He pauses when he gets into water over his knees, and I chuckle. "Perhaps just this far," I suggest, wading over to him. I am already up to my waist.

"It's not much of a swim."

I smile. "My legs are cold, Ekrem, and I don't really feel the cold. You must be freezing."

"Brisk," he says again, wading in deeper to meet me.

I gently put my paws on his shoulders when he reaches me, the water at our hips. "You don't have to do this for me. There's no sense in you freezing in this water."

"But I want to," he responds, putting his paws just above my hips. He smiles warmly at me, even though there is a little shiver in his chest.

"Ekrem…"

"Yes?" His eyes sparkle in the moonlight.

I lift my handpaws to the back of his neck and gently lean forward to kiss him. He returns my affection gently, and I feel alive. I feel loved.

"You are too kind for this world," I say when I break off.

He laughs. "Life is better when lived with kindness and compassion."

"I know, it's just … well you know how it's been."

"I am not afraid, if you're wondering."

I want to say he should be, but that's not the truth. "Perhaps I am then. There are things afoot I cannot control."

"There always are," he offers, ears perked toward me. "Living things fear. If you still fear things, then perhaps you are not so close to death as you think."

My ears shoot up, and I catch myself. "Indeed. What makes you so wise?"

"There are slow days at the store, and I read to pass the time. I listen to what people say."

I ruffle the fur on his sides. "You are special."

"Now you're just trying to flatter and seduce me."

"I've already got you naked."

He smiles coyly. "This was my idea."

"I almost feel set up then. You haven't got any vampire hunters or troubadours lurking in the bushes, do you? Will this be my end or will someone come out and sing to us about courtly love as we stand here in this pond?"

"It's just us, and I don't think I have the stamina to stand here for an entire rendition. My paws are freezing."

I laugh and let him go. Taking one of his handpaws, I lead him over to the shore. We brought towels and we dry off our legs and tails, then lie in the grass on the shore, clothes still neatly stacked next to us. I look up at the sky and the moon, bright and full above me. Ekrem curls up next to me, and I listen to his breathing. After a few minutes he dozes off, and I lie there thinking about him, and what I can do.

The night is calm, the insects singing nearby unconcerned about us. Ekrem's breathing is steady and relaxed. The beating of his heart, which I can just barely hear, is the one thing that mars this perfect moment. It is the one thing that reminds me of who I truly am, but still if I push that observation away, this is bliss. This is true happiness. I could get used to this.

I wait for a bit, watching the moon and stars shift before I wake up Ekrem so we can return to Strasek. Perfect moments cannot last forever.

❧

When we returned from the pond, I made sure that Ekrem went to bed. I cannot let my nocturnal habits keep him from resting. I've been reading before dawn comes, but nothing of note has come up. I did learn a lot about the intricacies of milking cows from the account one of the local farmers left behind, but that's not a skill I see needing right now. The diary does comment on a disturbance in Strasek that sounds like what I'm looking for, but it's only mentioned in passing.

Now I'm pondering again what I can do. There's so much I don't know, so much I have missed. The sun will soon trap me here and leave me bound in this house, a prisoner of its power.

Idly I pick up Katarina's journal and flip to the blank page at the back. She knew more about what happened to me, and what happened in Strasek, but what is it? What did she see? I have no way of knowing without the second volume.

I sigh and go downstairs to the back room of Ekrem's store to use the writing materials there. Ekrem has a dip pen on his desk, and I look at it carefully. Katarina wrote all her entries in this book with a quill, and yet such instruments fell out of favor years ago. Now business is conducted with metal nibs, and the best pens come from Birmingham in England. How times have changed.

I open the journal to the blank page, pick up the pen, and dip the metal nib into the ink on Ekrem's desk and write something in the back.

> *Oh sister, how I miss you. How I long to tell you what has happened these long years, and yet I can't. I put these words in the back of your journal so that whoever might read them knows that I loved you, and even all these years later, I still love you. I miss who I was, who we were, but time has taken it from me.*

I will find out what happened to you, and I will make sure what shadows prowl this village are put to rest. For the first time in a hundred years, I feel hope beyond just continued existence. I have once again found love, as weird as that makes me feel. Long have I carried this curse on my own, but now I have someone who sees beyond the shadows I have lived under. I know how things end for my kind, but Ekrem, his name is Ekrem, has given me my hope back.

And as foolish as I have been, I know I cannot bind him to me, and as time spins on, I will watch him slip from my paws. Yet, in this moment, can I not be content? I seek the power not to make more of my kind but to unmake those like me, and even myself. I hope as you watch me from the next life, you can take pride in what I'm doing now, and not who I have been. Finally, I am fighting back against the shadows. I wish it had not taken me so long to find this hope, but I am grateful that I have it now.

Your humble brother,
Radic

I set the pen down and look over the words. Perhaps they are too honest to leave behind for someone to find once this affair is over, but let them ponder the meaning and the strangeness of them.

Leaving the book open, so the ink can dry, I get up. I could go upstairs and join Ekrem in bed. The dawn is coming soon, but I do not wish to put a burden upon him, nor wish to make his bedroom my new tomb.

Instead, I head for the basement door, so that I might rest safely in the dark, and yet as I descend the stairs, I feel a strange warmth thinking about him. It will keep me safe this day.

As the Night Darkened

It is dark and damp when I wake up. Rain has blown in, and a strong earth smell pervades the basement.

I go upstairs, but Ekrem is not there. Instead, a note sits on his desk, on top of Katarina's journal. The book has been closed. I take the note to one of the windows on the second story, so I can read it in the fading light of dusk.

Gone to Tarcsa. I am glad to have brought such life to your time here. I will try not to skip all the way there. Likely back late.

Since Ekrem is not here, I decide to keep the house dark, and I light no candles. My dark vision is good, but I can't read in this gloom. However, even were I to sit and read right now, I don't think it will help. Yes, we have more old journals I can look through for clues, but the chance of finding something in them seems remote. Yes, I want to check them all, but so far, I've had no luck. Additionally, it feels intrusive to read about the mundane lives of people long gone who I know only through their words.

In a way, I am a prisoner of the curiosity shop, cut off from the wider world; without Ekrem, all the knowledge of the day is beyond my grasp. Perhaps I should leave and return to Vienna. I have connections there, and a place to lay low in an abandoned crypt that surreptitiously connects to the sewer system. Whatever smugglers built it are long gone, but what kind of life is that? I live like a rat under one of the greatest cities in Europe, carefully coming out at night to feed. For the last hundred years, I've lived in caves, sewers, and abandoned basements, always careful to have other nearby safe spots available. I've rented rooms before, but money is difficult when you cannot work a job like a mortal. I have learned it is better to hide and not need many guldens to get through my day to day.

I had to carefully plan for my trip to Strasek and acquire the coin. I sent the trunk ahead, to make my stay comfortable, and to sell the appearance of a well-off traveler. I know I could have more. I could easily hunt the city's streets at night and take the coin of my victims, but bodies always bring investigators. I've seen it happen before to other vampires, and I refuse to be foolish in my choices. The crypt has been my home now for ten years, and it has served me well.

I shake my head and get up from where I am sitting in the dark by the upstairs window. There is no point in going over my inconsequential life. I need to find out what Ekrem has learned, and since it may be a while before he returns tonight, I can at least hunt and feed. Better to be useful to myself than be useless to us both.

I have to go downstairs, to get the dip pen in order to write a response on the note. I leave the paper where I found it on the desk. Satisfied, I go up to the bedroom to undress and fold my clothes, laying them aside. I then silently slip open the window.

The moon is now starting to wane, so the change into bat form takes just a bit more effort than it took yesterday, but

I've never had difficulty doing it. It just takes more thought when the moon wanes to coax the change out of myself, but even on nights when there is no moon, I can make the transition.

In my other form, I take flight and leave the house behind. I feel the freedom of the night lift me up as I head out into the dark sky to seek a meal that won't bring the hunters upon me. There's something about feral creatures that is just different from us, and I can taste it in their blood. Without them though, I'd long ago have been found.

❧

A little over an hour later, I return to the shop, having fed on some feral deer I found in the woods. There is a light upstairs in the curiosity shop. I enter through the open window silently, then transform with a thump on the floorboards.

A moment later, I see the familiar face of Ekrem peeking into the room.

"I was wondering how long you would be gone for," he says, coming up to me. I can smell food cooking from the kitchen.

"Not long. I just needed to eat," I respond. "I trust the trip went well?"

"Not exactly," he says. "Things in Tarcsa are unsettled. I think I also met the woman you heard about in Herzok."

"This mysterious wolf?" I'm about to put my trousers on, but that catches my attention, and my hackles go up.

"Yes, but let me fix my dinner. Also, I have something for you."

"By all means, let me not keep you from your meal," I say. He takes my paw and I follow him into the main room of his home, my clothing forgotten.

At his hearth there is a pot hanging, and Ekrem seems to be making a simple porridge. A hard sausage sits on the table. He lets go of me to go over to the hearth to stir his food.

I, in the meantime, take a seat at the dinner table. "Tell me what happened," I say.

His ears flick, registering my voice, but he keeps his attention on the pot. "The journey to Tarcsa was pleasant, but as I approached the town, I felt as if I was being watched. The villagers looked at me suspiciously, as if I bore ill intent. Passing through the village square on my way to the castle, I saw a wolf by the well who appeared to be drawing water, but as I passed her, I could see she held a dowsing rod. Whether you believe such things work or not, you do not need one to find a well."

He pauses to stir the porridge. I watch him, and when he's done, I motioned him to go on. "And?"

"She turned and the rod pointed at me, so she spoke to me. 'Do you know what fate sees for you, my child?' she asked me. I of course told her I did not, but she smiled then, flashing her fangs at me and then she spoke. 'You walk in shadow, and yet you do not know it. You walk in the sun, and yet the night grows ever nearer to you. The hunt has only just begun, and already you are caught in the snare.'"

I frown. "Riddles?"

"I would think so, but she got close to me then and whispered into my ear that she could sense the corruption upon me. At that point I tried to walk off, but she followed me, prattling on about if I knew anything about the attacks and I needed to guard myself against the night. She only left me alone when I told her I was from out of town and had not been to Tarcsa in months."

I think about the exchange. Does my mere presence near him cause my curse to rub off on to him? Perhaps it is because some of our interactions have been carnal in nature. "And after that?" I finally inquire.

"She went back to stand by the well muttering to herself, and I continued up to the castle. It took a little cajoling, but I was able to get into the library and archive of the Dragomirka family. The librarian was not forthcoming to let me in, but when I told her I was looking for information about old legends possibly related to the attacks, she ushered me inside."

"You directly asked?"

Ekrem starts spooning his food out into a bowl. "What was I to say instead? Please let me peruse the archives unescorted? I had to give them enough to let me look around without arousing suspicion. She told me she herself thinks it's a vampire, but it could be a ghost or a spirit of some kind. There had been another body found in the morning, and the entire town was on edge. There's also tale of a specter stalking the woods, a bear who hunts the woods at night."

I suck in my breath. "That's likely the same one Katarina wrote about."

"I know. As for the books, I found a few things of interest," he says, pointing to his carry bag sitting on the floor. "You can go and grab them. I didn't get any lunch, so I am quite famished."

"Of course," I say, getting up to go over to the bag. Inside I find two books. Both are leather bound, and one is much older than the other, the leather well worn. This one has the title *The Study of Rare Medical Conditions* on the spine in flaking gold leaf, and I understand immediately why Ekrem brought it. The other is titled *Carpathian Folktales*.

"Folktales?" I say, turning to Ekrem.

"Yeah, they're from all over the mountains, but some are from this area."

"Oh, that is useful," I respond.

"Hopefully there are some clues in there. I didn't have time to go through it in detail. *The Study of Rare Medical Conditions* actually talks about vampires, although not in great depth. It's the only thing I found that directly referenced them that seemed to have any scientific basis to it."

My ears perk and I go over to the armchair as Ekrem puts food on the table for himself. "If you don't mind?" I ask, tail wagging eagerly.

"Of course, of course," he says.

I put the books on the table, but before I sit down, I walk over to where he has seated himself by the hearth. "Let me at least thank you for this," I say, tail still wagging.

He looks over at me. "You're welcome?"

I chuckle. "If that's all you want."

"Are you always so…" He waves a paw at me.

I have taken up a pose right in front of him, and I'm not even wearing clothes. "Forward? Excitable?" I pause and give him an amused laugh. "Not at all, but you've captured my attention. You can go places I can't."

He smiles. "I'm glad I can help. You are quite the handsome character to have around the house."

"I appreciate the compliment. I'll go through the books while you eat. And…" I gesture at my nude form, "I can put some clothes on."

"I don't mind you like this," he says, his tail softly flicking back and forth.

I think he likes me naked more than I like me naked. "Oh, well perhaps after dinner I can give you a little dessert."

His ears blush and he nods. He goes back to tending his meal, and I go over to the armchair in the back of his small room. I sit down, feeling the velvet of the chair rub against my nude backside. On a table by the chair is a candlestick, and I light it so I can see the text clearly.

I decide first to start with the textbook. Just from looking at the cover of *The Study of Rare Medical Conditions*, I can tell the volume is quite old, even older than me. It has two metal clasps keeping the cover shut, and opening the book to the title page, I see it was printed in Augsburg in 1683.

Idly, I begin to flip through it, getting a feel for what's inside. Most of the book seems to be pretty dense, and some of the diagrams it has suggest practices that even with my lay knowledge I know are no longer conducted, since they don't work. Flipping to the back, I'm pleased to see this thing has an index, and scanning it, I find vampirism on the list, referenced in two different sections. I turn to the first and begin to read.

Early church teachings claimed that the vampire is a creation of Satan, made to turn the bodies of those creatures who have forsaken God into hell spawn. However, in this age of enlightened animal kind, I believe such nonsense lies best in the past, and that there must be a scientific explanation, even though the affliction is supernatural.

Unfortunately, subjects willing to let me study them have been few, and my attempts to help one vampire resulted in me having to fight for my life. As best I can tell, the bite transmits something akin to rabies to the victim, but it does not induce the loss of the mind like rabies. On the contrary, vampires show standard intelligence, and ones that live a long time can accumulate far more knowledge and wealth than the average person.

However, the extreme sensitivity to sunlight and the need to feed on fresh blood excludes all but the most cautious from many years of undeath. The origin of the disease is unknown, but it appears to have existed across recorded time.

Because I have found no willing subjects to treat, I can recommend no cure for this disease. Some aspects of the affliction are apparently supernatural, but as I said earlier, the bite itself transmits similar to rabies. It is rumored the ancient pagans had a way to treat the disease by purifying the blood, but I have been unable to find any details on it. Treatment with fennel seems to help victims who were not drained of all their blood, but only rest seems to prevent the onset of the disease. A blood transfusion might help the victim, but such devices remain rare. Treatment for the vampire itself remains unknown, and death of the vampire is the only known cure for undeath itself.

The mention of blood transfusions surprises me, but such devices do indeed exist now. I could bathe myself in fennel perhaps, but I doubt that would do anything. I would have tied garlic to my nose if I thought it would have helped me, but the smell makes me deathly ill and repulses me now.

I flip to the second passage and scan it for where vampirism is referenced and find a short section.

While investigating uses of the old charms and tinctures used before this enlightened age, I have found reference to a special charm made by sorcerers and sorceresses composed of nine worts said to be able to cure things even as extreme as vampirism through proportioning the humors of the body. I have been unable to find the exact composition of the charm, and I can only assume that such medicine, if it ever existed, likely died out with the arrival of the church. While I am intrigued by the possibilities of these worts, I suspect the promised cure was nothing more than a trick played on the gullible and desperate.

Well, that doesn't help. There are manuscripts dating back to the early Christianization of these lands, but such texts are extremely rare. Even if I could locate the appropriate text, unless someone has translated it and published it, I am unlikely to be able to read one. My Latin is limited to knowing the chants and psalms I heard in church growing up, and my Greek is also limited to a rudimentary understanding of the passages from the Byzantine Rite the local priest still used back then.

The Imperial Court Library might have what I need, but Vienna is still a journey away. While we can easily access those, it won't be until winter when the days are much shorter that I myself would be able to go before they close for the day.

I sigh and close the book to contemplate it for a minute. Vague conjectures written before I was born are not going to help me, but the author at least considered treatment for my condition. Others must also have, but finding anything from them could take me years.

I set the textbook aside, pick up the folktales, and begin to read. Maybe there's something in the old stories I can use.

 ❧

"Is it time yet, Radic?"

I look up from the book of folktales. They've been enjoyable, but I haven't learned anything useful from them. The candle next to me has been burning down quite a bit. I must have been reading for a while. Ekrem is across the room, leaning against the wall. He has undressed now and is waiting for me expectantly.

I smile and put the book down. He walks over, takes me by the paw, and I get up, following him toward the bedroom. Ekrem lets go of my paw once we're in the room, and he gets on the bed, lying back, smiling up at me. In that moment, I feel suddenly vulnerable. I don't deserve Ekrem. I am hardly worthy of him.

"Are you sure?" I whisper.

He only nods in response, and as I approach, I can hear his blood quicken. It calls to me, enthralling me, binding me to him. Vampires can seduce, but my cautious diet has taken that away from me. Instead, I have been enthralled by him, and the promise he holds for me. The hope of more. The remembrance of what living entails.

A lubricant is of course at hand, and I am already hardening even before I lift his legs. He doesn't complain about my cold touch and the ice inside of me. I lick my fangs hungrily, wanting everything he has. His tail lashes in anticipation.

I do take the time to slick myself up, and slick him up with a digit, but my hunger for him is urgent. "Now it is time," I whisper, and he shivers as I position myself to sink my shaft into the leopard. His heat warms me, while my ice pierces him. He doesn't mention it, and only in the back of my mind do I wonder why not. My need only grows, and his heart races, drumming out a tune for me.

Ekrem cries out in pleasure, writhing in ecstasy, and I thrust urgently into him. I need this, and he is desperate. In the heat of my passion, only the hunger for our satisfaction remains. I forget what I am, and I think only of us, of love and needs splashed in sticky seed upon him and in him.

All too soon, he cries out as he climaxes, and I do too. Looking at the satisfaction in his post orgasm state, the trail of seed across his stomach, everything comes slamming back to me, and a thought strikes me. I could turn him. I could bind him to me. This little store could be our castle, until I lose him to time, but I don't have to let him go.

Yet as I look down at him with reservations about myself, Ekrem looks up at me blissful and tired. I don't know if he really understands my struggle, or if he'd let me feed a little from him. He might even let me take everything, if I asked, and that worries me.

I could claim him finally, binding him to me. If I turn him, he will be mine forever.

Instead, I only lean down to nose at his chest fur, scenting him, feeling the life within him. Oh Ekrem, what do you see in me? I am so wrong for you. I am so lost. Even though you're trying to give me back what I've lost, you deserve more. You should not suffer like I do.

"That tickles," he whispers, spent and happy. In his bliss I feel as if I've somehow reclaimed my soul, somehow stolen a piece of my old life back, even as I know how carefully I must tread to keep that from being a lie.

Playfully I lick his chest, feeling content, before gently pulling free of him and settling down next to him.

"You should rest," I say, and he yawns in agreement. He takes my paw again and rolls over to snuggle up against me, trying to pull me around him. I let him and lie there, my arm draped over him, happy. Content. Alive.

It is a perfect moment, except for his heart, still beating in my ears. I fold my ears back and try instead to focus on his breathing as he falls asleep against my cold body. When he shifts my mouth grazes his neck, but I only lick at him lovingly, even with my fangs right there.

I refuse to be the monster I was made to be.

Embers of the Fire

Once I make sure Ekrem is fast asleep, I carefully slip out of bed. He moves a little when I do but settles back down. He doesn't seem to notice my absence. He is so innocent and vulnerable-looking lying there, and here I am so full of shadows and half-remembered secrets.

I turn and pad carefully out of the bedroom into the living space. I might as well go back to reading. There's not much else I can do with the hours left until dawn. It's too risky to go to Tarcsa without a place to spend the day or the time to get back.

Picking up the book of folktales, I open it to where I left off and settle back down in the chair. I could dress first, but I like the way the chair rubs up against my fur. I'm sure Ekrem has a furniture brush I can use tomorrow to get some of the fur off I'm leaving behind.

As for the folktales themselves, they are amusing, but none of them seem at all related to my condition until I find one titled, "The Hunter." The title means nothing to me. The story is short, but when I read it, the words snap into focus because of what they're about.

Many years ago, during a time of great war, a hunter, desperate to feed his starving family, set out into the woods in search of game. He traveled for days, but he found nothing. The war had driven away all the game from the land, and so the bear returned to his village, heartbroken and hungry.

However, upon his return, he found the village under attack and ablaze. The hunter took up his bow and dagger and fought bravely. He slew many enemies, but he could not reach his home before his wife and two children were slain. Only when the dust settled could he find her — an arrow in her back, their children dead at her footpaws.

The remaining villagers tried to comfort the bear, but the hunter would have none of it. He went out into the woods again, alone and broken. He wandered for many days, with no set direction in mind, and only his tears, bow, and dagger with him. During his wanderings he stumbled upon a small cottage, deep in the foothills of the mountains. In it there lived an old woman, a fox with fur of silver. He was going to pass the cottage by when she saw him and called out to him.

"Why do you stalk my home?" she asked, fur standing up.

"Forgive me, baba, I only happened by here. I do not mean to darken your door."

"You do not hunt?" asked the fox, noticing he carried a bow and a dagger.

"I hunt no more, because there is no one left to feed."

The fox looked at his haggard and gaunt appearance and could see the truth in his words. "And why have you given up hunting?"

"The war has taken everything from me I hold dear. I could not protect those I loved. Now they lie dead, and I have nothing to offer anyone in my village. If I could not

protect my family, how could I protect them from this awful war?"

The fox beckoned him closer. "I can give you the strength to protect those who cannot protect themselves, but the cost to you would be great."

The bear considered for a bit, looking over his shaggy pelt and the ribs sticking out his side. "And what use would I be in this shape?"

"I have water most wonderful in a spring nearby, and I will give you a sip. It will restore your vigor, but you must use this strength to protect your village and these lands from those who would take it from us."

The bear agreed, and the fox gave him a sip of the waters, and the bear was indeed restored to his health. He returned from the woods, to protect the village. He built a lookout tower upon the hill above the village, and he guarded the village from there. When the war ended, he started a new family, and as a sign of his gratitude the villagers built a stone keep to replace the watch tower. The Huntsman was happy, but only with time did he learn what the fox had done for him.

To give him the strength he would need, the fox had given him a sip of the waters of life, and after that encounter, the hunter never aged. Eventually, when everyone he knew in the village had passed away due to old age, the hunter moved out to the woods, so as not to disturb the villagers with his agelessness. His children continued to live in the keep while the Huntsman lived deep in the woods. When trouble came to the village, he was there, fighting for them. No enemy could pass through the woods that surrounded the village without him setting upon them.

Even today they say the Huntsman is still out there in the woods around Tarcsa, watching for trouble while his ancestors still inhabit the keep he built.

By the time I finish the story, my paws are shaking, and I have to put the book down. Dawn is coming, but I want to fly to Tarcsa right now and risk everything to find out if there is truth in this tale. It can't be coincidence that something is happening in that area.

Tomorrow, I will go do my own digging around there.

❧

I awake just before sunset—which surprises me. I can feel that burning globe's presence still above me, but I'm safe in the basement of the store. I spoke to Ekrem just before dawn and told him about the story. We agreed I will meet him just outside of Herzok after dark, and he will have my clothes with me. That way we can go to Tarcsa together and get the most out of the trip. The nights also are slowly getting shorter as summer is approaching, and it limits my ability to interact with people.

The shop is deserted, but I cannot go upstairs until the sun sets. When I do, I can see a sign hanging in the window of the shop in the fading light saying it had closed early. Carefully and silently, I climb the stairs to the top floor.

The drizzling rain from last night has left everything damp, and I don't want to leave the window open with us gone. I pull up the glass and look around to see if anyone can see me. The street below seems deserted, so I crawl out the window, balancing with the claws of my footpaws against the steep slope of the roof, gripping the windowsill with one handpaw. I manage to get the window down most of the way before it sticks. I have to yank to get it closed, and that is when the motion of pulling it down dislodges me and I slip on the roof in a clatter of fur.

"Shit!" I yell before my common sense comes to me. My footpaws shoot out into nothingness, and I can feel myself falling backwards. I panic then and will the change—

desperately flapping my arms. I'm already falling before I can get wings under me and beat them. Somehow, I manage to get enough air under me to keep from hitting the ground in my bat form. I have to beat my wings hard to gain altitude, and moments later, a wolf comes hurrying by carrying a lantern in their paws. It looks like the town watchman is still on edge from the attacks that occurred here, and he glances around suspiciously. He doesn't seem to notice the bat flapping hard above him, but he investigates the street carefully and calls something out into the dark. I stay high, trying to watch him as I arc over the roofs.

After waiting a minute and checking for any footprints in the alleyway, he continues down it to the next street in a hurry. I can only breathe a sigh of relief, orient myself, and take off for Herzok.

❧

The day must not have been too warm, because it is only just past nightfall and fog is already starting to form. Herzok isn't hard to find since I'm following the road, but the night is going to be heavy and thick.

Finding Ekrem isn't hard either. We agreed to meet at the first bend of the road east of Herzok he felt was out of sight of the village. It only takes me three twists and turns to see him waiting by a fence, a lantern resting nearby. The area seems deserted, so I change back and land quietly in front of him.

He jumps, surprised at my sudden appearance, before he gets his composure. "You make great time in that form," he remarks. "It's only a half hour past sunset. It took me over an hour and a half to walk here."

"It makes travel faster, but the lack of clothes is a problem," I say, motioning for the bundle under his arm, which he passes me.

"Indeed. Get behind the tree while you dress."

I do just that, and after a minute I emerge presentable. Unless someone saw me, it looks like I came all this way like this. Ekrem motions and we start walking.

"Sorry for cutting your day of business short today," I apologize.

Ekrem holds up the lantern a little higher so he can get a good look at me. "It's fine. Sales have been modest the last few weeks, but I generally do rather well. I read that story myself after you went to bed, and I can see why you wanted to get here. You think it connects directly to the attacks?"

"It's hard to say. We know something happened in Tarcsa and it seems the Dragomirka family has a connection to the Huntsman. Plus, you saw that wolf there."

"I know. I thought about that, and I think we should rent a room in Tarcsa. I know a place."

I tilt my head to look at him. "A room?"

"Yes. Just something modest. It's a little too far to make the trip back and forth quickly. It will make it easier for you to look around, and Tarcsa is a market town. I can conduct some trade."

It's then that I notice he's got a pack slung over his shoulder.

"Don't you need a wagon with goods for that?"

Ekrem smiles and pats his bag. "If I wanted to purchase stuff. Right now I've just got some old cutlery of pure silver I took as barter a few months ago that I've been meaning to sell."

"I didn't know there was a robust market for silverware in this area."

The leopard laughs. "There's not. It's why I've been sitting on it, but if anyone asks what I'm doing, moving old stock is a good excuse."

"Do many know you in Tarcsa?"

"Just the traders. Tarcsa is a little too big for everyone there to know everyone, but I'm sure many recognize me."

I nod. "I trust your judgment on where we can stay and not be noticed."

Ekrem doesn't offer anything else, and we walk into the thickening fog toward our destination in silence. Tonight is a night for hunters, and while we seek answers, others have to be out tonight too, looking and seeking. Some might be seeking the other vampire, but I'm sure most are out seeking me.

☙

By the time we reach Tarcsa, the fog has come in thick as I expected. The road just winds its way into a cloud of nothingness. We pass fields where we can't see the houses of the farmers or any light. The waning moon is somewhere up above us, but invisible. Without the lantern, we'd be almost blind, but it creates only a little pocket of safety.

"I don't like it," says Ekrem. "Nights like this hide so many things."

The growing fog has made me nervous. Scent is far more useful than vision for finding someone on a night like this, and anyone tracking us could easily do so without us even noticing them. We increasingly have been in our own world as we've walked. "It does," I finally say.

Thankfully, a few minutes later Tarcsa eventually looms out of the nothingness that the fog creates, and I can see the leopard relaxes a little, his tail uncurling. He leads us to a coaching inn off the main square that is built with half-timbered construction. The sign over the door has a goose over it, the name, The Snug Pond, below it.

As we approach the door I pause, feeling the resistance since I have not been invited here. "Can you go see if there is a room?" I ask Ekrem.

"Right," he says, and I wait outside for a few minutes, trying to pretend I'm taking in the air, before the leopard comes back. Even before he does, I can feel the resistance to my entry ease.

"I got us a room," Ekrem says, coming outside. "The innkeeper was all too happy to give us a room, although it only has one bed apparently."

"That will do," I say, and I follow Ekrem into the inn. I wave at the innkeeper behind the bar, and the lynx waves back at me. This inn has a small common room, although it is not too busy right now. I see tradespeople eating their dinner, but not much else going on. As for the room, it's simple and plain. It contains a large bed with a straw mattress, a wash basin, and nothing else.

"It's at least serviceable," remarks Ekrem, looking over the bed.

I sit down on the bed. "This is what I grew up sleeping on until my family was wealthy enough to afford feather mattresses when I was eight or nine. I must confess, your cotton stuffed mattress is quite nice. They seem to be very common now."

"Thanks, and they are. Although for now, I guess this will have to do."

This room is on the second floor, and conveniently located next to a set of stairs that descend to a back door leading to the yard. The room does have a window looking out the front, but it has old wooden shutters. I get up to check them, and I see they close pretty tightly. Satisfied, I turn to Ekrem who is now sitting on the bed. "I should procure some graveyard dirt for myself, and a sheet to put it down on."

"Is that necessary?" he asks me.

"Usually, if I want to rest. I feel so comfortable at your house I don't need it, but I'd like something to ease the tension in my tail."

"Perhaps some wine?"

I shake my head. "Alcohol doesn't really do much for me anymore. I just tolerate it. The social aspect of drinking is what I enjoy." I stretch, feeling the coiled tension in my body. Just because I don't age, doesn't mean I don't get cramps. "Do you think you can find some cloth tonight? I'd like some for the window and something to cover myself with and keep the dirt contained."

"I can do that. The general store hasn't closed yet. They should have some cloth for sale, but where are you going?"

"The fog hides many things, does it not?"

"It does," Ekrem says.

I smile, flashing my fangs. "Then it can also hide me. It's time to do some hunting of my own."

Whispers of the Past

Foxes, by their very nature, are hunters. My feral ancestors were hunters, and while we are so much more civilized now, we still carry the fangs of a predator. Since I was turned, mine have become stronger, and they can lengthen now, but they have always been part of me.

Foxes also are not the strongest of God's creatures, but I have never felt weak—or, at least, not in a long time. Yet the virtue I need tonight is not strength but stealth. I have no idea where the answers I am looking for are, but they're here. They won't come easy though, so that means I need to turn over some stones.

The fog's moisture settles into my fur as I walk down the street. Somewhere above me, lost in the milky dark, is the castle of the Dragomirka family. If I'm lucky, their records and the story they tell are likely locked away in the castle's stone walls. If I'm unlucky, they're no longer here. There is the question also of whether they contain what I need or not. However, that doesn't mean I'm powerless to find these answers.

The road to the gate is deserted, but I follow it anyway through the fog. The cobblestone street crosses a bridge to reach the gatehouse. Two heavy, ancient, wooden doors bound in iron seal the way. While it looks like there was once a drawbridge here, the entrance has been rebuilt not to require one. The need to defend the castle is no longer necessary, and it instead serves as a family seat.

This fortress may no longer be guarded by a watch, but that makes entry no easier. The gatehouse is at least twenty feet off the ground, and the castle walls are still steep. Even up close, I cannot see the entire structure in the fog.

Which also means no one can see me.

I backtrack to the other end of the bridge and start to climb down. The rock here is rough, and doing it in the dark, even with my excellent night vision, does not make it easy. I slip once, cutting the pad of my paw on the sharp stone. Precious, irreplaceable blood leaks out. I want to lick it all up, but it's mixed with dust and dirt.

At the bottom of the cliff, under the bridge, it is a little dryer. I undress and neatly fold my clothes up. The damp immediately seeps into my fur in places usually protected. When I am finally naked, I shiver, not because I am cold, but because I am nervous. Even with the fog, a naked red fox in the seat of the Dragomirka clan may not go unnoticed. Still, I am doing this for a reason, so I step out from under the bridge and will the change upon me.

Sailing through the fog now on membranous wings, I can feel the heaviness of the air and taste the earth below me. I still cannot see the castle well, but this body can sense things in the dark, and I use that to sail through the blinding mist and over the ramparts.

The castle is quite sizeable and built upon an outcropping of rock. While fortifications like these are no match for cannon fire, it is still quite formidable. I follow the outer ramparts around to get a sense of scale of the place, and

I realize this is not a small castle. The lower ward seems somewhat unused, but the inner ward appears well kept. At the heart of the castle there is a large keep, to which a large hall is attached. Flying over the structure, I can feel the push of the chapel against me, consecrated ground I cannot enter.

I look for a part of the wall that has a good view of the inner courtyard, and I land there, turning back into myself.

I swivel my ears back and forth to listen. In the fog, I can hear nothing. Everything is still, and yet there's something about this place that feels off. There is the chapel pushing me away, but there is more than that in the air. I've never been here, and yet there is a strange familiarity in my corrupted body, as if these walls echo it back to me, almost welcoming me. It occurs to me that since this is a residence, I shouldn't be able to enter the castle, and yet I know I can before I even try.

I shake my head, confused. Whatever calls out to me, it cannot be good, but I do not need to trick my way in. I had hoped the library would be a separate structure that would admit me, but now I see I can go wherever I please here. Even the chapel, if I pushed hard against the consecration, might admit me. This lack of resistance to my entry means I can explore the grounds to find out where the books are kept.

I scan the ward below, trying to see if any signs have been hung for visitors, but the fog is too thick. The rampart I am on forms one side of the outer wall of the castle. Looking out beyond the walls, I don't see anything; the fog swallows all. In the keep, I can just barely make out light in the windows, and by the gatehouse between the wards, a lantern has been hung that has been lit. Beyond that, the inner ward is deserted and empty.

The section of the wall I landed on is the only part of the inner courtyard that doesn't have any structures built against it. The rampart looks like it runs all the way to the main keep, but someone is in there. After a moment of consideration, I change back to my bat form, beat my wings, and then glide down to the courtyard before turning back into myself.

I crouch down and again I check for sounds, but I hear nothing. The stone of the courtyard has a familiar feeling that I recognize. I can tell someone is interred here in the castle walls because of the way the ground feels. As I listen, I can feel the damp tugging at my fur, weighing my tail down, and yet it is this soup that will keep me safe. It is the only armor I have.

Looking over the U-shaped inner courtyard I can get a sense of how this place was built. While all the buildings share walls, each is distinct. On one side of the keep there is a chapel. The other side has a large hall that butts up against the keep. It appears newer and has ornate stonework that is different from the other buildings in the castle; I suspect it replaced an older structure. It could be a ballroom, great hall, or something else. On the other side of this hall is a series of smaller and narrow buildings that look older. The last one abuts the wall between the wards. Rising next to the gatehouse between the wards is a sizeable tower that serves as a strong point overlooking the lower ward.

The archives is likely in one of the smaller buildings. I really should have asked Ekrem exactly where before I decided to do this. I start to move toward the door when I hear a sound coming from the gatehouse, and I notice light is coming now from the passage between the wards.

I change back to my bat form and quickly beat my wings rapidly to gain elevation. Flying over the inner ward, I turn to parallel the wall that divides the two wards and see who might have seen me.

Emerging from the gatehouse into the inner courtyard is a single figure: a well-dressed lynx carrying a lantern and a parcel of some kind. I can't tell who they are, but with the finely detailed yet restrained cut of their clothes, I think they're a manservant.

I circle above the castle as they go toward the keep and enter through the main door. I wait a few minutes, but they don't reemerge, so I swoop down to land by one of the doors into the smaller structures.

I can only hope no one notices me as I approach the door. Over it is the crest of the Dragomirka, but there is no sign. However, the larger windows in the front of the building do seem promising, so I try the door. Surprisingly, the bolt lifts easily, signaling the door is unlocked.

If I still breathed I'd hold my breath. Instead, I stand there naked in the fog with an ear pressed to the door, the latch engaged, but the door still closed. Again, only silence.

I open the door slowly and the well-oiled hinges swing open smoothly. I step inside the building and then slowly close the door behind me. The latch makes a soft click when it engages again, and I stand naked in the darkened room.

Outside, it is dim, the light faint. The fog has swallowed up the starlight, but in here it's even darker. The meager light entering from the window is so scant I can't see anything, but my nose tells me I've chosen well. I can smell paper, and there's a lot of it.

There's got to be a lantern or a candle nearby. Stepping away from the door, I use my other senses to find my way through this space. My claws echo against the stone, and I start working out the fainter scents in the room. I can just make out the back wall, and I'm so focused on that, that I miss the desk in front of me and slam right into it.

Everything on the desk shifts, and I hear something metal topple and hit the stone floor. There's a crack, and then the sound of whatever I just knocked rolling away from me. That suspiciously does sound like a lantern.

"Oh, that hurts," I grumble, taking a moment to collect myself. I hope no one heard that, but I pause to listen. Then, I get down on my paws and feel around the floor for whatever just fell. The item turns out to be wedged under the chair, but this does prove to be a lantern. Unfortunately, I seem to have damaged the glass, because I nick my handpaw just picking it up. Now I just need to find some way to light it.

Getting back on my footpaws, I start to feel around the desk. I feel an ink well, a dip pen, and a book of some kind, but no matches. The only source of flame I have is the lantern outside. I'd need wood, or something else that I can burn in order to light this lantern.

Tracing my pads across the desk, I grab a piece of loose paper. I retreat to the door with it and the lantern. Carefully, I open the door and stick my muzzle back outside.

The inner ward is still deserted.

I really don't want to do this but I need a source of light, before I take out some more furniture. I quickly carry the lantern toward the gate. Checking by the lantern to see if there's anything on the paper, I can see in pencil a note on it that says, 'refill ink bottles in morning.'

Well, that won't matter since everything on the desk is now disturbed. I open the glass shade of the burning lantern and roll up the paper. Carefully I light the end of the paper, and as the sheet curls up, I stick the sheet into the lantern I'm holding. The wick catches easily.

I drop the flaming paper on the wet flagstones. It sputters, but it looks like it will burn up. I turn down the lantern and walk back to the door. Compared to the mess in the entranceway, this bit of ash won't be noticeable.

Reentering the building with light, I can see this is an entrance hall. The desk I investigated in the dark appears to be some type of check-in desk. Looking at the book on top, it is a log for visitors and what books they've checked out. I see Ekrem's name on the last used page. Off to one side is a set of ornate doors, and then two smaller rooms on the other side. A set of stairs lead up. The strongest smell of paper seems to be coming from the large set of doors, so I go over there and push them open to peek inside.

I expected something nice, but not like this. Beyond is a large two-story room with wooden beams framing the ceiling. Against the back wall there is a large hearth and a clear space. The rest of the walls are covered in ornate bookshelves only broken up by space for the windows. A second set of shelves have been built above the ground floor shelves served by a wrought-iron catwalk. A ladder leads to the catwalk. Tables for reading fill the center of the room along with some comfortable armchairs.

This room exudes wealth and power; the shelves are full of books. I could let myself get lost exploring these shelves. It will take quite a bit of time for me to find anything in here. I'm sure similar titles are grouped together, but I'll have to read the spines in order to learn how the room is organized.

Also, my lantern will easily be noticeable through the windows. Who knows when or if the lynx might pass by. Ekrem has already been here looking for material, so what I really want likely isn't in this room. This is a public space. If the Dragomirka have collected such an ornate collection of books, there must also be a private archive here.

I retreat back to the entrance hall and look at the other two rooms on this floor. One seems to be a bindery for maintaining the old volumes in the library, and the other is an office. I peek around there, but I don't find anything that catches my interest. Upstairs though, is another hallway. One door opens to the main part of the library and the catwalk built into the bookcases in the great room. Another room has a collection of shelves that seem to have volumes of various ages with simple spines. There's a final room on this floor, but this first room looks promising.

I set the lantern down on a table nearby and start to look over the shelves. I see one shelf that has the names of villages in the area and years on the spines, so I select one of the volumes to investigate. This proves to be a list of names with dates of birth and death dates. It's a copy of church records, and the next book on the shelf I investigate is the same. It doesn't take me long to locate records from Strasek. I take a moment to find the volume containing my birth and am easily able to locate it. I also find Katarina's birth and my death recorded in the book. There is no note about the missing body by my name.

Replacing the volume, I look further, and am able to find tax documents along with other assorted records. On a different case, I find a set of volumes with the Dragomirka crest on them, and opening one, I see it is a chronicle of some kind with dates and short entries. Unfortunately, it's in Latin, and it takes me a few minutes looking over the page to puzzle out that this appears to document events at the castle. Whatever truth there is to the legend of the Huntsman, it could be here, but turning to the first page and just trying to read the inscription makes my head hurt. My Latin is not up for reading something like this and outside of a few words, I can recognize nothing.

The neat cursive words stare back at me, almost mocking me. The truth of how this castle was founded and if the Dragomirka have a connection to the curse is in these books. Everything I want to know I hold right here in my handpaws, and I cannot read any of it. Ears drooping, I close the book. I trace the pad of my paw across the leather cover, thinking. There are other volumes with the family seal, but all the old volumes will be in Latin like this one. As far as I know, Ekrem doesn't know Latin either.

I'm snapped out of my reverie by the sound of wood creaking. I flick my ears up and swivel trying to find out where the sound came from.

There is silence for a few seconds, and then I hear something move in the hallway outside, as if someone is on the stairs. There's another creak, and a softly uttered curse.

The room I'm in has a lock, but even if I lock the door, whoever this is could have a key. Gently, I put the book down and reach to turn down the lantern so it goes out. Perhaps they won't come here and I can —

There's another creak of the floorboards, and this time it sounds closer. They're still coming upstairs, and under the door I catch a flicker of light.

My only hope of escape is the window, but I cannot get it open without making a sound.

I wait and the light under the door becomes steady. Then I hear the sound of keys.

There is no time; I run toward the nearest window and yank desperately to pull open the window to get outside. There is a sudden commotion as I hear paws scramble on the floor outside toward me, and I just give up and throw myself against the wooden frame in frustration.

Glass shatters and cuts me, but I manage to force the latch and open the frame. I can hear the door to the room open and light from a lantern floods the space. By then, I'm practically falling out the window as the transformation takes me.

"I knew it," a woman screams, but I'm already soaring across the courtyard, pushing up with my wings, I manage to climb and turn. I look back at my pursuer.

The wolf has charms braided into her fur, little bits of silver, and she watches me like a hawk as I cross the courtyard, a scowl across her muzzle. There is an intensity in her gaze, her eyes boring toward me in the dim light. In one paw she holds a dowsing rod. I push up and over the castle walls and she vanishes from sight.

I'm not sure if she saw me clearly, but I need to get back to Ekrem. It may not be wise to stay here. She might not have seen me as a fox, but her nose is likely sharp. She'll know I was a fox.

❧

I change back to my normal form. My clothes are still under the bridge, and I dress quickly. I hear no pursuit, so I climb back up to the road. The distant gatehouse, barely visible in the gloom, seems dark but who knows for how long. She could come out of the castle at any moment, so I walk back into town in the fog. It quickly swallows me and I lose sight of the castle.

Alone in the mist, I will be safe. All she has to go off is I'm a red fox. Foxes are common in these parts, so while changing forms does tend to leave behind a few stray strands of fur, it will really depend how much of my scent she picks up with how easy she can track me. The dampness should play in my favor.

That and the dowsing rod, clutched tightly in her paw.

I stop for a moment and a chill seizes me. Ekrem said the rod had pointed at him and she said she could sense the corruption on him. She wasn't looking for water by the well. She was looking for the presence of vampires, and the rod had pointed at Ekrem. Wherever she was in the castle, that dowsing rod drew her to me. The inn will not be safe for me. Ekrem could stay, but I need to go back to Strasek tonight. She'll certainly have questions for him if she does find him.

I can feel my mind reeling at the thought. Something is going on here in Tarcsa, but it is not safe to stay in town. Maybe I can find a nearby cave to hide in, but I wouldn't know where to begin. No, we need to get out of here now. Scouting for a cave will have to be for another night.

I try not to run back to the inn, but walk purposefully. The night is quiet. Reentering the inn, I see things have calmed down. I wave to the innkeeper who gives me a look. It's not unfriendly but there's a little frown. Going upstairs and then down the hall, I knock on the door to our room. When I hear no sound, I let myself in.

"Ekrem, are you awake?" I ask.

He's sitting on the bed and looks concerned; then I hear a click behind me from a voice I've only heard once before. "Close the door slowly and turn around."

I don't need to turn around to know who this is. Lorelei has found me.

Ties of Blood

I close the door and turn toward her slowly. In the shadows of the room stands a fox, her crossbow raised and at the ready. The iron at the tip of the bolt catches a little of the light from the small candelabra on the wash basin.

Ekrem is sitting on the bed, frozen. "Lorelei, I can still—"

"I'll deal with you in a minute," she interrupts him. "I warned you about getting involved with him, so now this is my problem to deal with."

I consider the distance, and if I can reach her before she pulls the trigger on the bolt aimed at me. It's not a big room, she's only a few feet away from me, but it will certainly cause a disturbance which will bring the innkeeper here. This could get messy quickly.

She's young, somewhere in her twenties or early thirties, and her fur is well groomed. She's wearing a simple but practical dress that suggests she's a farmer, but her crossbow looks well maintained and carefully oiled, just like a hunter's. Next to her is a pack, and I get the sense the bolt has been blessed in some way, as I can feel it gently trying to push me back.

"You have me at a disadvantage," is all I can offer in the face of this ambush.

She smiles, showing her fangs. "It's taken a couple years for me to meet you, Radic Horban. You're not the type of man that's easy to track down. I thought you might still be in the area, but Ekrem insisted you moved on. Now, I see that someone has been lying to me."

The leopard pipes up from the bed, "He's not who you think."

Lorelei gives Ekrem a disdainful look. "I know exactly who he is."

I spread my paws. "And who do you think I am?"

"A vampire, and quite an old one at this point. You're cleverer than I thought. The trick with the cows isn't something I've heard of before. It's only because a farmer told me his cattle had been acting strangely tired after Alina died that I found out about that."

"I'm not sure if that is a compliment or not."

She shrugs. "It's why I have never been able to track you. Unlike every other vampire I have encountered, you don't leave bodies behind."

"Bodies create questions," I say. "Questions become problems."

She smiles, her tail wagging a little. "That they do. So, let's start with that. Who killed Alina?"

"I didn't kill her," I say.

"I know. I looked at the cows. You're too precise to leave marks like that."

"I don't know who they are, but I think I ran into them three nights ago near here. They didn't leave bat form though."

"That's a clue. Who bit you?"

"I don't know who they were. They never stuck around to tell me."

She frowns, and her ears flick back and forth. "No name?"

"If he told me, I did not remember. The stoat used his powers of suggestion against me, and I was brought under his spell. He led me to my fate."

She considers. "Interesting. The one Ismail saw was a weasel."

Since she's not immediately trying to put the tip of that crossbow bolt in my chest, I decide I can press her. "So, I've heard. Now it's time for a question of my own. Where's Katarina's diary? I've seen the first volume, but there's a second, and the only way you know so much about me is if you have it."

She shifts on her feet. I've caught her off guard. "What's it to you?"

"She was my sister! You have no right to it."

She laughs slowly. "Ah, you are as naive as I thought you were. Well, I have just as much right to it as you do, but you won't find what you're looking for in there."

"That's for me to determine," I say proudly. "As the last Horban, I deserve answers." It's bravado, but maybe she'll respect it.

She lowers the crossbow a little "Those journals belonged to my grandfather."

"Your grandfather?" I say, looking at her.

She nods. "Gavrilo."

I open my mouth and shut it as she looks at me defiantly. She can't be.

"Does that name have some special meaning?" asks Ekrem.

"Yes," says Lorelei. "He was Katarina's son. Radic is my great-great-uncle, and my family's greatest secret."

I stare at her in disbelief. I never thought I would encounter a relative. "You came all this way to put me to rest and tie off the end?" I ask. How much pain have I brought to the family I don't know about?

Lorelei's ears flick back, but she keeps the crossbow pointed slightly down. "If I must, but you are not my greatest worry. There are things afoot, and I'm going to get to the bottom of it. I'd have tried harder to find you if there were bodies, but there weren't. It looks like I will need you."

I quirk my ears. "For what?"

"We'll get to that. I haven't decided if I trust you or not."

"Well, family relationship aside, the feeling is mutual," I say. "You hunt my kind."

She snorts. "With what most vampires do, do you blame me?"

"No," I say. "I've seen what the hunger can do."

"And you've succumbed to it, I'm sure. Maybe not now, but in the beginning you did. There's blood on your paws."

"He's not a killer," interjects Ekrem.

She glances at the leopard. "Every vampire is a killer. Radic too. He is repentant perhaps, but he did his share."

I growl at her. "It's been ninety years since I've drank from a sapient creature, but I take it my attempts to reform and the struggle with my curse are not of interest to you."

She focuses her attention back at me and considers. "I want to believe you, but it's not easy to trust you. I've seen what your kind do. No matter how much you struggle, the curse still holds you. Knowing that, how can I ever really know that I can trust you?"

I could protest, but I'm not sure what proof I can really offer her. "You won't."

She smiles again, flashing her fangs at me, and there's something about it that unnerves me. "Exactly, but there is a way," she says, fishing out a flask with a cork stopper from inside her cloak while balancing the crossbow in the other handpaw.

"What are you doing?" I ask.

"Stay there," she says to me, and then looks at Ekrem. "You, come here."

Ekrem gets up from the bed and walks over to her. "You'd have killed him already if you didn't think you could trust him," says the leopard.

"Perhaps, but do you really believe that? Are you willing to put your life on the line for that faith?"

The leopard pauses, tail lashing. "I don't understand the question you're asking me, but Radic will not hurt me."

"I realize the question seems obtuse." Lorelei says, as she lowers the crossbow. Using the handpaw of the arm that's holding the crossbow, she pulls the cork stopper loose from the flask. "For your sake, I hope your faith is well founded."

"I don't unde—" He doesn't finish before Lorelei has lifted the flask up and dumped the contents on top of Ekrem. Immediately, the scent hits me. It's pig's blood, just like Ekrem got from the butcher. I can feel my eyes widen, as Lorelei drops the flask and raises the crossbow.

I cover my nose with my paw and turn away.

"Look at him, Radic. Tell me he's not a tempting meal for you," she commands me.

"He's my friend!" I snarl at her.

"Look at him!" she says again, raising the crossbow. "Or I'm going to put this bolt into your chest."

I turn to face Ekrem. The leopard looks shocked and disgusted. He has curled his tail around himself, yet a trail of red has run down his face. In his eyes I can see confusion, but in my ears, I can hear the rapid heartbeat of prey.

"You could sink your fangs into him right now," she says.

The smell of the blood is stale, but deep down it is tempting. It's always in the back of my mind, and while I don't want to take Ekrem, I can feel my fangs stir. Below its promising scent, there's something more. There is fear, and that fear is because the stale blood covers a delicious meal—

"Radic … please…" says Ekrem hesitantly, his tail has curled under himself.

And I hear two hearts beating. One is calm and collected, the other frantically calling to me, asking me to take everything it has, to feed and suck its vessel dry. He would be tasty, oh so tasty, but I know the cost.

I turn to look at Lorelei. I am not that fox anymore. "Is this how you hunt? You use innocents as bait?" I ball up my handpaws in fists. "Well, I will not be so tempted."

She just holds the crossbow level at me. Seconds tick on, and she doesn't say anything. Finally, she lowers the crossbow and slides the bolt off. "So I see."

"I am covered in blood," hisses Ekrem.

"And you are alive," says the fox. "There's water in the washbasin. Go clean up."

I watch the leopard walk over to start scrubbing. "Why would you do this to him?" I ask.

There is a playfulness in her response, one that I recognize almost as my own when I was young, but it also has a seriousness about it. "Because I need to trust you have control over yourself for what is coming."

"And what is coming?" hisses Ekrem, as he's busy scrubbing his fur clean.

"There are other hunters after Radic, but they don't want him dead. They want him alive."

"The woman in the castle with the dowsing rod?" I ask her.

Lorelei's ears lower, and her body language shifts. "She's here? I thought I'd have more time."

"Time for what?" I say.

"Wait, did you enter the castle?" Lorelei asks. "Why would you do that?"

I frown. "They have an archive. I found a folktale about the Huntsman that suggests the Dragomirka family are related."

"And you entered the castle freely, uninvited?" Lorelei presses me. Her fur has suddenly fluffed up. This fact alone seems more concerning to her than my existence.

"There was a bit of resistance, and yet a familiarity to the place."

Lorelei takes a deep breath. "Radic, this is incredibly important, but did you ever visit the castle while you were alive?"

I think. "No. I honestly don't recall going to Tarcsa much. There just wasn't a reason, and back then the castle wasn't open to outsiders."

She sighs. "Well, I know who bit you then, and if Bianka saw you, she knows exactly who you are. Get your things; we need to go."

Ekrem looks up from the washbasin where he's scrubbing congealed blood out of his fur. "What?"

"There isn't time. Clean up and come on."

❧

After he gets himself not smelling like pig's blood, which takes far longer than Lorelei wants it to, Ekrem grabs the pack he brought. We exit the inn from the backdoor and cross the coaching yard to use the carriage gate.

"Is this truly necessary?" he asks, as Lorelei unlocks the gate.

"We really don't have time for this."

Ekrem crosses his arms. "I'd like to know why we're leaving a perfectly good room to wander around in the dark without a specific destination in mind."

She has partially opened the gate and is peeking outside but closes it to respond to him. "Fine, but let's stick to the most important parts, and discuss the details later. I hold an imperial writ issued in Vienna, that allows me to hunt vampires throughout the empire. My crossbow is a symbol of my office, although few know such things exist. However, since this area is part of the Kingdom of Hungary, imperial authority here comes from Budapest, not Vienna. The Dragomirka have authority to issue their own laws under the imperial court in Budapest, and Bianka operates for them. Her authority is absolute in matters such as vampires here, and I must follow the local laws."

"And why does that matter?" I ask Lorelei.

"Because she has the authority to talk to the burgomaster and call the local constabulary up. She doesn't want to kill you, Radic. She needs you alive."

"Why does she need me alive?" I ask. "You've not been clear on this."

She sighs and looks at me. "You read the folktale about the Huntsman, did you not?"

"We both did," says Ekrem.

"The wise woman, hag, or just elder in the folktale, whoever she was, gave him a sip of the water of life. Whether it's true or not, his blood conferred immortality. Many have searched for the water of life and never found it. But drinking sanguis vitae, the blood of life, the blood of any vampire, also confers immortality. The Huntsman is not the only source of the vampire curse, but the Dragomirka seek the blood of their ancient ancestor, and if you can enter their castle uninvited, you carry that within you, Radic."

The sense of familiarity. I am bound to them through blood like I am bound to Lorelei via blood. "Wouldn't any vampire do?" I ask.

She shrugs. "I would think so, but nobles want what they want. Your blood is a fine wine to them, and locked away in their dungeon it could be harnessed to make members of their family ageless."

That makes me shiver. "I am once again prey for someone," I whisper.

"We all are," says Lorelei. "Our feral ancestors were both hunters and hunted by others, Radic. Even a wolf is prey if they are sick and weak. Civilization has changed things, but it has also made us all prey for the powerful."

"That's not a comforting view on life," remarks Ekrem.

"I live in Vienna. I know enough about the imperial court to know it's full of powerful hunters, seeking their whims," she says, opening the gate. "Let us make our exit from their clutches while we still can."

I consider. "Wait. Do you want me to just follow you two in the air?"

Lorelei stops. "You know that's not a bad idea."

I start undressing by pulling off my belt.

"You can at least turn around before you do that!" she hisses.

"Sorry," I say, ears going flat before I can turn around. I hand my clothes to Ekrem as I take each piece off. "Call out for me when you want me in my fox form," I say, and then I'm a bat and once again pushing up through the air on membraned wings.

੶

The farmhouse Lorelei leads us to is a small structure with a barn surrounded by a fence that looks like it's seen better days. It is quite a way out of town, off a little dirt lane. While Lorelei calls for me, I circle it twice before I decide to land to change back.

"This place is safe?" I ask her.

She turns her head away from my naked form. "As safe as you're going to get, though you'll have to sleep in the root cellar," she says, pointing to a small structure half buried in the ground. "I wasn't exactly expecting to have to put you up when I rented it."

I curl my tail around myself to give me some modesty. "I appreciate that," I respond. Ekrem comes up and hands me my clothes. I take that as my cue to start dressing.

"How did you know where I was?" asks Ekrem, as I'm slipping my trousers back on.

"I didn't, but I saw you buying sheets tonight. It's a bit strange to find someone who doesn't live in town buying bedding, so I just followed you back to the inn. It wasn't hard to guess why you were doing it."

"Figures," the leopard mutters.

"So why do you need me alive?" I ask Lorelei, now that I'm presentable again.

The other fox looks me over before I respond. "You don't realize how unique you are, Radic. Vampires are cunning, but they need to feed to survive. Those who have amassed great wealth can hide their crimes and walk in the shadow of the night for years undetected. Few though have directly tried to confront the curse like you have and tried to manage it like a malady, at least that I know of."

"So, to you I'm just a curiosity?"

She starts walking toward the house and I follow. "No. It's more than that. To finally put the greatest secret of my family to rest would close so many loopholes, and yet I did not know before I met you if I should."

She pauses at the doorway, and then enters the house, leaving me outside. I walk up to the door, and trace the wood frame, feeling that same feeling of familiarity I had at the castle before I entered.

I enter and Ekrem follows. This house is small, with only two rooms. One is a living space and kitchen while the other is a bedroom. It's furnished sparsely.

Lorelei nods at me. "No resistance?" she asks me.

I shake my head.

"I suspected there wouldn't be because of our blood relation," she says as she lights a candle on the table in the room.

"So now that you've met me?" I ask.

"You are even more of a mystery. You are a lone hunter who strikes very carefully and subtly. That's something you learned how to do, I imagine?"

I squint at her. "Since I'm hoping to dissuade you from trying to stake me, I'm not sure I should tell you what the hunger was like back then."

That elicits a laugh from her. "I'm honestly curious how you've come to manage it so well, but perhaps later. There are much more pressing things to discuss." She motions for Ekrem and me to sit at the table.

"Would you like something to drink?" she asks Ekrem.

"Some wine," he says.

"I've got some."

"I'll have a glass too, so as not to be the odd one out."

Her ears shoot up. "You can stomach wine?" she asks.

"Yes, but it doesn't do much for me. Red would be best. It's the only real food I can handle and enjoy."

"You are even more curious," she says, fetching some earthenware cups and a bottle. She sets them down at the simple table and sits down.

"Why do you keep calling me curious?" I ask. "I've heard of other vampires drinking wine."

Lorelei pours out the dark liquid from the bottle. "It's my understanding it's not common, but the research is just not there. I've learned all sorts of ways to kill you, but very little about how to coexist with someone like you."

I give her a low growl. "Does this mean when this is all over you will put a crossbow bolt in my back?"

"Only if you give me reason to." She picks up the goblet. "Katarina always had hope for you to come back to her, to have conquered this curse. My grandfather and father passed down her journals because they knew she longed to find the truth, but you must have come across one of her earlier journals. We only have them from after you died."

"I found it in the shop," says Ekrem. "Uncle Ismail probably bought it as part of a bulk sale and kept it. He had trouble throwing out things like that, or, well, really anything at all it seems. I've found things like chipped plates no one would pay for."

"I guess we're lucky he didn't. I'd like to see it, if you wouldn't mind."

I glance at Ekrem. "I can swap volumes with you. In that thread, what happened to Gavrilo?" I ask. "Katarina said there was a specter of some kind in Strasek."

"There was. I know about that. As for Gavrilo, he died forty years ago in Klosterneuburg, when my father was still young. He had a family late in life, but he passed down the journals. Dad says he didn't like to talk about what had happened much. Gavrilo stayed in the family trade as a vintner, and that gave him stability."

That was my destiny, before the curse had been laid upon me. I'd been finally acquiescing to my parents' wishes, and then even that had been ripped away from me. Klosterneuburg is close to Vienna also. I didn't know he'd been so near to where I was.

"So, what happened?" Ekrem asks.

Lorelei takes a gulp of wine and gets up. "I'm still piecing that together."

I look at her, confused. "What do you mean, still piecing it together."

She gets up and goes over to a bookcase and picks up a book with a dusty cover off a shelf, similar to the other journal of Katarina's and comes back. She hands it to me. "The journals don't answer all my questions, but I've figured out more than Katarina seems to have, or at least more than she was willing to say. You might make more sense of some of her thoughts than I have." She sets the book on the table in front of me.

I pick up the journal and examine it. All the pages are here. "What are you hiding, Lorelei?" I say, looking up to squint at her.

"Some would say ours is a cursed bloodline, but I think we have just seen behind the veil more than others." She pauses to take a sip of her wine. "I need to stop Bianka, and the Dragomirka clan. You also are not the only vampire in the area. If Bianka captures either of you, she will turn you over to them. I suspect both of you were turned by a man named Mathias, and his progeny are the only source of the precious bloodline they seek. However, I cannot be completely sure the other vampire came from Mathias. You though, definitely did. As for Katarina, she's the one who killed Mathias."

That gets my ears up. "Vampire hunting runs in the family now, I see."

She chuckles. "It does seem so. Now, why the specter of the Huntsman has appeared again, I don't know. Why the other vampire came back here, I don't know either."

"It could be coincidence," says Ekrem.

Lorelei fishes a small necklace out of her pocket with a gold signet ring threaded through it. She tosses it to Ekrem. The leopard catches it and looks it over. "It's not," says Lorelei.

"The seal of the Dragomirka family?" he asks.

"Yes. It was stored with Katarina's journals. Dad found it when he acquired them. I recognized it as a ring pertaining to a noble house, but I didn't think much of it. As far as I know, we don't have any noble ancestors, so I assumed it was probably a memento of a suitor of hers when she was young, before she married Gavrilo's father, Leopold. It was only recently I learned which noble house the insignia is from."

I frown. "Leopold was a nice man, but he was no noble. He died of a fever just before Gavrilo was born. I was at his funeral."

"He also was a fox. The Dragomirka are all bears. So, the mystery I cannot work out is why was this with her personal papers? Dad and I weren't born in this area, but Gavrilo was. He knew which noble house this seal belonged to."

Ekrem looks over the ring again, and slips it onto a digit, where it hangs loose. "It looks like someone had a big paw."

"Right, but whose ring was this?" says Lorelei.

"You know the answer to that is likely in the castle, somewhere in the archives, along with where the Dragomirka came from. I was in the castle looking over their records. They kept a chronicle."

Her ears go up. "Really? I'd like to read that. I doubt they're just going to let me do that, especially with you breaking in tonight."

"Same. How is your Latin?"

Her ears go down. "Awful."

"Ekrem?" I ask.

His whiskers flick. "I knew a few prayers from church. That's all."

I pick up my wine to take a sip. "Well, the part of the archive I looked at before being found out was in Latin. At least the older volumes are, and who knows if they've changed over. So even if one of us could get in there, there's a good chance we cannot read any of it."

"The entire archive is in Latin?" asks Ekrem, his tail lashing as he thinks. "Why would they do that?"

"Latin is the traditional language of the church, and many governments once used it for their own administration. The Romans kept records in Latin in the west and in Greek in the east. I'm surprised though everything is in Latin," says Lorelei.

"Not everything is in Latin. The parish records and the tax records aren't. But the part of the chronicle for the castle I found is in Latin. It's all stored in a room above the book bindery for the library. It's not in the main hall."

Lorelei takes a long sip of the wine and sighs. "I'm sure Bianka has already warned them about leaving the archive open. Unless she thinks she can trap you in there, there's no way she'll let you back in there, Radic."

I open the journal. "And there's nothing in here about this ring?" I ask looking over the pages. I immediately recognize Katarina's name in the inside and her handwriting. Despite myself, I can feel my tail has started to wag.

"I've never noticed a mention of it," says the other fox.

I flip through the book. I see this is full of entries, and even if there are not any grand revelations in here, these are my sister's thoughts. Her hopes, her dreams, and all the years I missed, at least a piece of them are in here. This is the closest I can get to her now.

"Radic?" asks Ekrem.

"Hmm?" I say, looking up. I realize both of them are looking at me.

"You stopped paying attention."

"Sorry, I just … I miss her. I miss her a lot. I could have come back and said goodbye, but I didn't." I trace the pad of my handpaw across the pages. "My parents, Katarina, they're all gone. This, the other journal, and their graves, is all there is left of them. There were no photographs back then and we didn't have the money to travel to go sit for a portrait."

"Katarina did sit for a portrait later in life."

My eyes go wide. "Where is it?" I ask, looking around.

"It's not here. It's in Klosterneuburg," says Lorelei. "It's small, but it's hanging in my father's home."

"I must see it someday," I say, my tail wagging eagerly. As foolish as I know it is, I wish we could leave now.

Lorelei notes my eagerness. "She meant a lot to you, didn't she."

"Yes. If you don't mind, I'd like to read now," I say, holding up the book. My tail is still eagerly wagging.

"Of course. There's a chair and another lantern by the fireplace. I should get a fire going though and get some of this chill out of here."

"You must be tired," I remark. "I know Ekrem is. Get some rest. I'll get the fire going and keep an eye on it. I'll need to find myself something to eat later, but there's still plenty of time before dawn."

"It has been a long day," says the leopard.

She considers, pondering something. "That's fine," Lorelei says finally, getting up. "I've got a cot for you, Ekrem."

While Lorelei is getting that set up for him, I go about making a fire in the fireplace. It's been a long time since I've done this, but I manage to not smoke up the house. I also make sure not to put too much wood in, since we just need a little heat.

Ekrem decides to sleep by the fire near me. Lorelei retreats to the privacy of the bedroom, but she leaves the door open. By the time I get the fire going well, Ekrem is already asleep. I watch the way he breathes, envious that he does even breathe. I miss the fact I no longer have life like that inside of myself. He looks so peaceful curled up under a blanket. Shaking my head, I sit down and flip the book open.

Dear Diary,

With a new volume, new possibilities are present. The world is bright and fresh after a rain this morning, and yet I can feel the growing sense of doom inside myself. I spoke to the priest today. What he told me has chilled me, and I must process things before I can fully record what has happened.

Know this though, dark times await Strasek, and I fear I will not be able to protect Gavrilo. I do not yet know if I even have the strength to protect myself, but I must. Few know what really happened to Radic, but I fear the threat lingers. What left the empty grave is not my brother. I cannot be sure he would not strike me down now like he was stricken.

And yet I hope wherever he is, there is peace inside himself, for death is a part of life, and without it, you live without possibilities. It is hope that will carry me forward these next few months.

IIdly, I wonder if the only reason Lorelei hasn't tried to kill me is because Katarina missed me so much. I haven't really thought about why she should trust me. I took the fact she hadn't pulled the trigger of the crossbow as a sign she was willing to talk. Now I realize Katarina always had hope for me, even when she faced the threat of Mathias. Since I've proven I have control, Katarina's feelings likely influence why Lorelei has decided to trust me.

Not only that, but she has also given me something special. Reading this book, I can reconnect a little with my sister. Also, on the topic of family, I should ask Lorelei more about what has happened to them all. There must be others besides her and her father. I'm not sure I can be involved in their lives, but it would be nice to know they're doing well.

Ekrem rolls over in his sleep, and I glance up from the book at him. Being here feels almost normal, like I've suddenly become a cherished grandparent. If only I could sit with them in the morning light, and not have my fur burn off.

Still here, in the night, as I flip to the next journal entry in Katarina's journal, I feel at peace.

⁊

A lot of what Katarina talks about in this journal after the first entry doesn't seem particularly important. It's very mundane, and I cherish that. Her entries after she visited the village priest seems almost as if she doesn't want to share what was said. She has an involved write up of recent business dealings father has undertaken, however, and how she's been involved. There's a section about how she is hoping Gavrilo can take over when he's old enough. And then there's an entry that does catch me off guard.

I once thought my life would be simple, but when Leopold died, I knew I would need to be strong. Father has continued to run the business, and I have taken to it since there is no one else to run it. A single woman has few prospects in society, but here in Strasek, many know my story. My husband died suddenly, my brother was brutally murdered, and if I do not take up the family business, who will? None question me when I show up representing our family.

I realize now that that this safety I've thought I've had is just a lie. I have known it for a while, but I have pretended not to see what I know in my heart. I was visited by a boar shortly after Radic died who wanted to talk to me about my brother. He spoke in a manner quite strange, almost as if everything was a riddle, and we danced around the true reason of his visit, as if he was trying to figure me out before he asked more serious questions. Finally, he got to the heart of the matter. With how Radic died, he told me it was likely he had been turned into a vampire, existing in a state of undeath. It was important if I saw him to not approach him and seek out the village priest.

I of course told him that was preposterous, that we had buried my brother. He asked then if the grave had remained undisturbed. I wanted to hide the fact it hadn't, but he read the truth from the position of my ears before I could catch myself.

I said whatever came out of that coffin was not my brother, and I did not know where that shade of my brother was. Afterward, he left, and I was left to ponder. What if that was Radic? What if he's still out there? If he is still my brother, why hasn't he sent word? I found the whole thing so shocking, I didn't even record it in my previous journal. I never saw the boar again anyway.

I remember what the priest told me three weeks ago, and what I've grappled with, not wanting to write it down. I know Radic rose, and he has not been seen here again. The boar who visited promised to kill Radic and send him to a final rest. I sat stone faced as he said that, but if my brother had been turned, what could I do for him? I told Ivan I wished him well, and he left. Three weeks ago, the priest told me that Ivan was killed. The details were not pleasant.

Wait, Ivan? I can feel my paws start to shake. I remember him. He tried to trap me, to kill me, but I killed him instead. I had been drunk on the blood of another kill, and I used my powers against him. I made him offer me his neck, and then I supped my fill. I left his husk behind after I had feasted, living off his lifeblood.

The priest says Ivan was likely killed by Radic. He'd been stalking a fox vampire, but the fox killed him, ripping into his throat, and drained him.

I had not learned restraint yet then. There had been blood all over my muzzle, but I had easily learned not to offer him a piece of myself and to bring my victims back. Even as I reveled in the kill, I refused to share this curse with anyone else. I did not seek out others of my kind till later, and even then, I always approached on equal footing.

I wanted to tell the priest it wasn't Radic, that it had been another fox, but I secretly believe it was. My brother has become the violence and death inflicted upon him. I do not know how much of him is still left, but not enough. I asked the priest if there was any part of Radic's soul left, and he told me vampires do not have souls anymore, that it has been taken by the curse. A true and final death may be the only mercy left for him, said the priest. My paws shake thinking about that, but better that than this hunger that grips him.

Last night, while returning home from work, I think I saw the spirit bear Gavrilo saw. It crossed my path, intent in pursuing someone it seemed. I tried to wave it down, but it spared me a glance before it moved off, warning me not to follow in a voice that surely comes from beyond the veil. This morning, I heard there was another attack in town, the body bloodless.

I realized these last four years, I've run from the truth. I've refused to record even all of it down! The cursed one that turned Radic is apparently once again hunting near our little village, and I realize now what I must do. The Huntsman still comes to protect us, to warn us about the dangers beyond our little village, but his power has been stolen away. He can no longer save us, so we must once again save ourselves from dangers beyond. I will answer the call both for Gavrilo and my parents to cleanse our family of this association. Yet as I contemplate taking up the mantle of the hunter, why do I still hope there is a piece of Radic left that could be pulled back?

I wipe the bloody tears from my eyes with my handpaw, staining the black fur. Katarina knew the depth of my sins.

She knew what I had become, and yet why did she still have hope for me? How could you still have hope for me, Katarina, when you knew what I'd done?

I close the book with a sob and put my head back against the armchair, my muzzle pointed up toward the ceiling. Blindly I stare at it, not seeing. My earlier feeling of peace is shattered.

࿔

"Radic, it's almost dawn."

I am jolted back to consciousness. I blink and look up from where I'm sitting in the chair. The journal is still clutched in my paws. Lorelei is standing over me. The other fox has an inquisitive look on her muzzle.

"I must have fallen asleep," I say, surprised at the fact. Ekrem is still on the cot nearby, fast asleep.

Lorelei speaks softly. "You did. I could have draped a sheet over you, but leaving a lifeless body in the middle of my lodgings does get a bit awkward. Plus, I do like to open the shutters."

"Sorry," I say, getting up and putting the book down. There is dried blood on my left paw. my blood, I shift to hide it. "I normally don't just doze at night."

If Lorelei notices it, she doesn't say anything. "Honestly, I didn't know you could just sleep at night."

"I usually can't. It's very rare for me to just sleep normally. I was just thinking about things."

"You're surprisingly sentimental for a vampire. Most are not," she says, starting to head for the door. "Also, you've got flecks of dried blood around your eyes."

I reach up to wipe them away. "Sorry, I was crying. I was reading and it got me thinking." I look at the book for a moment where I've put it down, before I follow her. "You knew I killed Ivan."

151

She pauses at the front door and turns back to me. "I did. I read the entire journal. That was a long time ago."

"Yes, but," I look down at my paws. "I killed him."

"You're a vampire, Radic. I know you've likely killed dozens of people, possibly hundreds."

I feel my tail curl up. "I did, and you know that. Why do you trust me?"

Her muzzle quirks up in a smile. "I also know the trail of bodies stopped. I'd have thought you dead, but when I saw you, I realized you very much were still here. I wondered for a long time about that, but when I saw the cows, I realized how you've been pulling it off. Still, I needed to know for sure."

"That's why you threw blood on Ekrem."

She shrugs and we walk out of the house. The fog is still thick outside and the air damp. It seeps into both our pelts. "I've never met a vampire who could resist it. The fact Ekrem is still alive tells me you're not the same person who killed all those people," Lorelei says, once we're walking across the yard.

"Yes, but I remember those years, the taste. It doesn't take me much to hear the heart beating in your chest and the song your blood sings to me."

She stops, and I can see her hackles have gone up. Her heart has started to race.

"The song never stops. I've just learned to tune it out. To ignore it."

"You hear it all the time?" she asks me.

"All vampires do." I close my eyes. "Your heart beats out a thrum of notes that I could find in total darkness. If I can hear, I can hunt."

I open my eyes to see Lorelei has turned back to face me. The sky is brightening. "You can do this with any animal?" she asks.

I nod. "Yes, but the blood of sapient creatures is what sings the loudest, what tastes the best. It's how a vampire can use the power of suggestion on them. I just live in a pale form of undeath because I don't drink the blood of sapient creatures."

She frowns. "I have a strong will. I think you'd have trouble doing it to me."

"It doesn't always matter if it's strong or not. Ivan had a strong will, but sometimes even a strong will can be bent." I think back to that night, so long ago. "I seduced him, called to him, and he answered. The mind can be influenced."

She takes a moment before she responds. "Are you telling me this because you want me to put the crossbow bolt through your chest?"

"No! I just..." I look down at the ground and my footpaws. "I hate it. I hate that I can do this to people. That you can just bend them to you. A vampire's power of persuasion is a dangerous weapon in the hands of one willing to use it."

"What about Ekrem?"

I look up. She's tilted her head to study me. "What about him?"

"He seems quite attached to you."

My ears go down. "He has been most kind. Perhaps a little too kind, but I have put no spell upon him."

She takes a deep breath. "Perhaps I should kill you, Radic, and be done with it. It is what I have done in the past, but Katarina never gave up hope for you. You'll see that later in her journals. That you're still here suggests her faith seems at least well placed."

"I did honor her faith, eventually, after I learned how to manage the hunger," I say. "Although it took time. Too much time."

"Many things do. I looked for you for a while after I saw you. I could only guess you might come here on the anniversary of your death, and I had written to Alina to let me know if you did come to this area. Still, I needed someone who could engage you directly. With that incident Ekrem and his uncle had, he was easy to enlist as a spy."

She pauses and chuckles. "Yet now that I've met you, I can see why Katarina kept such faith in you. As I said, you are unique among the vampires I have dealt with. None I know of have the control you do."

"I am pleased to have at least proven to be the man she wanted me to be." I consider for a moment. "How many vampires have you killed?"

"Six. None of my hunts have been easy."

The sky is becoming even brighter, and I can feel the warmth against me, even if the sun has not yet risen. "I wouldn't expect them to be. I can tell you I didn't make them. You have to give over a drop of your blood to make another vampire. I've never done that."

"That's good to know." She looks up at the sky. "The dawn is coming."

"I know." I say, walking over to the root cellar and pulling open the door. Inside there are stairs leading to darkness.

"There's some canvas down there if you need it."

I enter the stairwell leading down. The smell of earth is strong and overpowering. "Thank you, Lorelei." Then I close the door, and in the dark gloom descend. There's just a tiny bit of light that sneaks in, but it's not a concern. When I reach the bottom, I lie down on the cold earth, and I wonder what comes next. So much time has passed, and yet the scars I created are still fresh in my mind. I ponder that, but in minutes I'm out cold, dead to the world.

The Last Sunset

Sunset jolts me back awake. Sometimes I wake up gradually, but today, I have abruptly been released from my slumber, even though I lie in darkness. The tyranny of the day is over, and the moment the sun sank below the horizon, I awoke gasping silently. I am still here, still in this world, even if I probably don't deserve to be.

Lying in the dark and mulling over the entirety of my life, especially with the events of the last weeks, I wonder if I should ask Lorelei to put a crossbow bolt through my heart. Maybe my time is done. Destroying the bloodline will keep anyone else from gaining the immortality within my body, and I have crimes I have never paid for.

I sigh, feeling mortal, and pinch the bridge of my muzzle. No, I won't do that. Katarina had faith in me. Ekrem has faith in me. Lorelei has faith in me, even though I don't know why. I will have faith in myself, even if I am not sure what I can do to stop the Dragomirka family. First though, I should see what this new night brings.

Emerging from the root cellar, the sky is clear, and the first stars are already coming out. I take the moment to brush the dirt off my clothing and out of my tail. One thing I like about my tomb back in Vienna is it has all the feeling of a graveyard without any dirt getting into my fur. Sleeping on dirt is quite comforting, but it reminds me of what I've lost.

Entering the house, I see that it is dark, and neither Ekrem nor Lorelei are here. Tonight is much nicer than last night, the weather pleasant, but it's still a bit cool. I light a candle and then busy myself lighting the fire in the fireplace. While cold no longer bothers me, I've finally found family again. I would be remiss not to show my gratitude to Lorelei, and to Ekrem.

I get the fire going so it's warm, but not overpowering. I don't want it to be too big, since they don't need that much heat, but the light gives the room a nice homey feeling. I also notice there is flour and other foodstuffs here. It's possible I could actually cook for them, although I haven't cooked food in a hundred years. I'd either oversalt it or just burn it.

No, I should leave the preparation of food to them. On that note, I should secure some nourishment for myself. I'll do that when they get back. In the meantime, I sit back in the chair and pick up the journal to read.

I've opened back to the entry I read yesterday and flipped to the next one when I hear a sound in the distance.

I lift my muzzle up and rotate my ears. Someone is shouting.

Frowning, I put the book down and get up.

"Radic!"

I run over to the door and open it; there coming down the lane, running full tilt, is the leopard who has captured my lifeless heart and given it hope again.

"Ekrem?"

"Radic!" he yells, seeing me. "We need to hurry."

My ears go down. "Hurry where?"

He reaches the yard and comes to a stop, wheezing. "Lorelei..." He sucks in a deep breath. "Lorelei left this morning to go back into town. She wanted to get some supplies, like butter and coffee."

"Well," I say, starting to get nervous, "when is she coming back?"

"She was supposed to be back by noon, but she didn't show up. So, I went into town to see if I could find her. I found out she has been arrested!"

I blink. "Arrested? Arrested for what?"

He looks away from me. "Rumor in town is there was another vampire attack last night, this time in the castle itself. Apparently, they're charging her for working with the vampire."

"What?" My tail droops, and I feel ice in the bottom of my stomach. "I told you what happened at the castle."

Ekrem turns to look at me. "I was worried at first you'd turned, gone feral maybe, and that you've been lying to me. That this has all been a ruse."

No, this can't be happening. "Ekrem, you know I didn't kill anyone yesterday."

He studies me. "The badger who told me this at the inn said something about a fox who did this. They're saying the victim was a caracal who worked at the archive."

My head spins. "The building was deserted when I entered," I whisper. I'm still in control of myself, aren't I? I'm not losing my grip on reality, am I?

"There's more though. They said the caracal was working late, but the man who was telling me this found that strange. Said they hadn't seen this librarian in over a week. He'd heard he'd gone missing."

None of this is good, but I can feel my tail relax. I hadn't realized it had curled so tightly. He knows I didn't do this, yet he needs to be sure "Someone is laying a trap."

"It is, but that's not all. There was a second victim, also last night. The wife of a miller. Her husband said he saw a weasel. The whole town is up in arms, and they're pinning this all on Lorelei."

I let out a low growl. "They need evidence. What ties her to the castle?"

He scratches behind his head. "Everything I heard is second-hand, so I'm not sure. Supposedly they found red fox fur in the castle, and the Dragomirka apparently don't employ any foxes. I find that a bit of a stretch, with how big the place is."

I stamp my paw. "That's my fur!"

"I know. I'm sure they know that too."

I growl more and pace back and forth. "They're using Lorelei to lure me to them."

"Did Bianka even see you clearly?" he asks.

"Not sure, but I'm sure I left a little fur behind. It wouldn't have been hard to find it. Changing forms always does rough up my pelt."

"We need to do something. The head of the Dragomirka family arrived in town today, apparently. He's promised to sort out this matter and punish the errant vampire hunter."

I feel my chest tighten. "Did they say what they will do to her?"

Ekrem shakes his head. "I don't know."

I play over the scenarios in my mind. A town in the midst of a panic will accept the unthinkable. I've seen people desperate and starving turn on each other. I saw it during the uprising in Vienna twenty-five years ago that culminated after months of unrest—when the imperial army turned their cannons on the city. It's easy not to think about such things when you're undead, but the living face such panic head-on. The Dragomirka already have their scapegoat. They need to only manipulate the law to their needs.

But they also need the blood of a vampire, and not just any vampire. They need a vampire they don't have in their possession. We can use that against them, but how?

"Lorelei is in the castle?" I ask the leopard.

"I think so."

"Well, first thing is draw them out of the castle."

"How do we do that?"

"I'm pretty sure if I kill a few people and leave some bodies lying around, someone will show up when they find out, but that's bloody." I consider. "But … that could be exactly it!"

Ekrem looks at me, confused.

"Bodies attract hunters. Any vampire who hasn't just been turned knows that. This other vampire didn't kill just for food. They want to be found."

Ekrem frowns, ears flicking. "By the Dragomirka?"

I scratch at one of my ears. "Possibly, but if you wanted to see the Dragomirka, why not just go to them? No, I think I know who they're looking to be found by, me."

He doesn't say anything at first but just gives me a hard glare. "That could still be a trap," he finally says.

"It could be. Just tell me where the body was found, and I'll look."

"I'm coming with you."

"No, you'll be fine here."

"Sitting by myself? Hardly. I've still got the room at the inn, plus Lorelei left me something to defend myself with. Let me go get it."

He walks toward the open door of the house. I stand there for a moment, confused, before I follow him inside. "Ekrem, just tell me where the body was found," I say. By the light of the fire, I can see him opening a drawer of the desk inside.

"Just a moment," he says. "I need to load it," and that's when I realize what he's retrieved, as he pulls a powder horn out. Inside I see a cluster of barrels and a handle attached to them.

"She left you a pepperbox pistol?" I say, looking over the firearm as he pulls it out of the drawer.

Ekrem nods. "Lorelei told me if I needed a way to defend myself to use this."

"From me?"

The leopard shakes his head. Carefully, he tilts powder into each of the barrels. "I asked about that. Apparently, the crossbow works better against vampires than this, but she said it was just in case."

I feel like everything I love is slipping away. "Surely she doesn't think you need a gun."

He looks at me. "Radic, I've seen what a vampire can do up close. You forget that."

"Yes, but I'm just going to talk to them." I pause, ears drooping. "I think."

"And if he tries to kill you?"

"I'll fight back."

Ekrem is quiet for a minute. "And if the Dragomirka try to kill you?"

I look at my paws. I've fought with myself for so long to not kill someone. To be better, to not be seen or noticed. "I really hope that it doesn't come to that."

"I do too," he says, "But something is going on. We need to be prepared."

I look around the simple farmhouse with the warm fire I stoked and the armchair. Katarina's journal sits there, waiting for me to read more from it, for me to know what happened to her and Gavrilo. It is so peaceful here. Why can't I get that in my life?

I don't have anything to add, so Ekrem quietly finishes loading the pistol, adding a ball and a wadding to each barrel. Finally, he loads the percussion caps at the end of each barrel. Then he hesitates for a minute, looking over the powder horn and remaining supplies before he goes and gets his satchel. He dumps out the silverware he was going to trade, then puts the ammunition and powder into his bag, slipping the pistol in last.

I want to tell him he's being unreasonable, but I have a sinking feeling he's going to need that gun.

❧

Ekrem and I part ways at the edge of the town. He heads to the inn while I head to the mill. He said the body of the miller's wife was found downstream from the mill. This one is different than the one I visited with him two nights ago. It is built by a stream that naturally drops enough that no pond is needed to power the waterwheel. This mill is rather close to town, and I see the castle of the Dragomirka family up on the hill.

This building looks fairly new, and I can see people have gathered there from the scents and sounds I can smell outside. Friends and family likely paying their respects to the miller. I give the building a wide berth to follow the water downstream. It's a rocky stream too, and I am not even out of sight from the mill when a voice speaks to me.

"I warned you to leave."

There on a rock, across the stream, is a weasel. He's completely nude, crouching down, watching me carefully.

"Do I know you?" I ask.

"No, and I don't want you to know me. You just need to leave."

I frown. "Why?"

"They're looking for you, Radic."

The fact he knows my name is a concern. "I know that, but they're looking for you too."

"Ah, but I'm not the one who they think killed the innkeeper, that's you. You're the one going around pretending you're still alive. I have never let them see my face."

I feel my hackles go up. "Alina was a nice woman."

"One life to save many lives is no great loss. I've killed a lot of people," he says, and he tilts his head at me. "They all blend together after a while. Haven't you done the same?"

It takes effort for me not to snarl at him. "Not anymore."

He smiles, showing me his fangs. They're all the way out. "That's why the Dragomirka are going to drain you. That's why they sent their little errand girl after you. They want what's in your veins, not only for who you come from, but how you've been tamed. Your blood is noble, and nobles always want to keep their blood pure. That's why I tried to get you to leave."

Now that confuses me. "They plan to drain me?"

"Oh yes, every drop. They need every bit of you, but it won't matter if I do it first," he says, and smiles at me. "Go now, before I kill your leopard friend and that fox. I've never had leopard before, so don't give me a reason to sample him. Felines tend to have a wonderful spice in their blood."

I am quickly wishing I had brought the pepperbox with me. "So, you've been following me."

"No, that's too difficult, but Bianka has spies. She won't tell me who, but I can guess. It doesn't matter. I'll kill her when this is done and then leave," he says, standing up. "My blood is not noble. They won't spare me."

He pauses, ears swiveling when I hear a hunting horn in the distance. "Shit … they're coming!" He hisses. "I knew I only had a few minutes to talk to you. Go, now!" he commands, and then he changes.

The bat beats its wings, quickly heading toward the woods. I can hear voices and see light spilling out of the miller's house. I turn to flee, but emerging from behind a tree is Bianka, a crossbow raised and pointing at me. The small charms braided into her neck ruff glint.

The wolf curls back her lips, amused. She's just a little taller than me, but her presence feels impressive. "His mind isn't all there, but Einhart has done what I needed him to do. Don't think I'm about ready to just let you get away," she says.

She's ten feet away from me. "What do you want?" I ask.

She kicks over a set of manacles with a footpaw. "Put these on." Even with the moon obscured by the trees, I can see them glint as they land not far from me. They're made of silver or at least lined with silver. It will prevent me from changing.

I growl. "Get out of my way!"

She snarls back, and I lunge. She pulls the trigger, and the crossbow bolt grazes my shoulder. I don't lunge straight at her, hoping to knock her aside. The one time I'm not naked and need to transform immediately, and I cannot; I would immediately get tangled up in my clothes.

Bianka growls and swings the stock at me, catching me in the ribs as I try and get past her. There is shouting in the distance, but I shove past her and run as fast as I can.

"Oh no you won't!" she yells at me, but I'm already fleeing into the woods. Other voices are calling out, but my only hope is to escape.

All I can do is run, stumbling though the brush and rocks along the side of the tree. Twigs tear and rip at my clothes as I move through brush at high speed. I hear a click and a twang and the sound of a crossbow bolt burying itself into a tree trunk. I run through the dark, tripping, stubbing claws, but the shouting is behind me. When the stream drops into a pool over a small waterfall, I glance back seeing lights, and I make a snap decision: I dive.

The water is cold, like when I took the swim with Ekrem, but the pool is big enough that I can swim down. Clawing at the stones at the bottom in the muck and the dark, I wedge my handpaws against a boulder and then get one of my footpaws against something solid. Then I close my eyes and wait.

I no longer need to breathe, but submerged in the bottom of the pool, I feel suspended. I'm too afraid to look up since my eyes will reflect any light back to the surface. Seconds go by, then minutes, but all I can hear is the water from the falls. I think perhaps I hear footfalls, but I cannot be sure.

Finally, after what feels like an eternity, but could just be minutes, I open my eyes and try to see what is above the water. There is just darkness, so I push up off the bottom and swim up.

I emerge into the night and blink to clear my vision. No one is here. I can hear distant voices, but they seem to be moving away from me. I escaped her, but as I climb out of the pond, I realize my clothes are torn and ripped. I try and shake some of the water off of me, but I'm still soaking wet. If there is one thing about my feral ancestors I really admire and wish I had, it was the ability to do a full body shake like they do in moments like this.

My spare clothes are back at Lorelei's house. It would take me over an hour to get there and back, if I walk. Just because I gave Bianka the slip doesn't mean she's still not searching. While she might not know Ekrem is at the inn, she still has her dowsing rod.

While I'm debating, there is the soft beating of bat wings and a thump as the weasel lands.

"You were clever with the pond, but she'll see through you and double back."

"You again," I growl.

"Me…" he laughs softly. "Yes, me."

"So, you work for Bianka," I say, getting closer, appraising him.

He spits on the ground. "I work for her because I have to, not because I want to."

"She has something over you?"

"Ahh, not so dense as you seem. I had hopes. And yes, same as you."

"I'm not in the mood for games."

He chuckles, circling me slowly. "But you are in one already. You are the prize. I am not."

I turn as he tries to walk around me. "My blood is no better than yours."

He chuckles. "To us. To anyone else, but not to the Dragomirka. He took some of my blood, but yours is the one he wants. He promised my relatives will live if I give them you."

I frown. "Then why try and scare me away?"

"Because I know why the Huntsman is here, and it's not for me. He's here for you."

"What?" I say, confused.

"You! All you, not me!" Einhart laughs, until he sees my expression and then shrugs. "You get bored when you are kept in a cage for so long. You have to invent new games. She showed you the manacles, didn't she? They'll be yours if you stay. I'm tired of wearing them anyway."

The weasel carries himself as if he's almost feral. It's unnerving, but also confusing. Something about him feels broken.

"Look, I've got to go save my great-grandniece, so I appreciate the warning, but I'll figure it out."

"No!" He grabs one of my handpaws and pulls me to him, seeming almost desperate now. "You must listen. They took her because they want you. You must leave."

"I know if they capture me, they'll kill me," I say softly.

"Foolish, stupid, so stupid!" he says, although the way he says it almost makes me think he's talking to someone else. He closes his eyes to steady himself. "Fine, go be a hero, but I cannot buy you much time. You must leave and never come back to this area once you get her. Promise me that."

"I…"

Einhert's eyes fly open. "Promise! Please. Please," he says, getting close to me. "Trust me."

I look at the face and in the dim light, his eyes reflect sadness at me. This close to him, I can tell he's suffered in some way. Also, it's then that I realize his fur is warm.

He notices as my gaze falls down to his paw. "Ah, now you realize a little what they've done to me."

"How?" I ask, holding his handpaw, feeling how strange it is. His heart does not beat, and yet the feeling of life is infused into his fur. What did they do to him?

"It's too long a story to tell you." He lets go of my paw. "Just know it's painful. It hurts. It always hurts."

My mind races, playing out what might have happened to him. "Bianka did this to you?"

He shakes his head. "No. She is a pawn herself, but she knows she's being played."

"By whom?" I ask.

"The Dragomirka, of course. Well, one Dragomirka— that fool Friderik. He did this to me, and he wants your noble blood back." The weasel pauses. There is shouting in the distance coming back this way.

"The hunters are coming back, go!" he says, breaking off the contact with me. "I'll create a distraction, but Bianka will know it's not you. Go!"

And then Einhart dashes off, toward the stream, leaving me confused. I can hear him purposefully moving through the dark woods, trying to catch people's attention.

Confused by the encounter, I make my way carefully back toward town. I'm not sure how I'm going to explain to anyone what a sopping wet fox is doing around, but I first need to get there.

I hear no sound of pursuit though, and I reach the first houses on the outside of town with no problem. I find a barn nearby, and creep over there to get my bearings and figure out my next move.

Ekrem is in the inn, but I'm not currently presentable. Since I'm all wet, I would draw attention to myself, but I need to get to him at some point. This point becomes especially important if they're actively looking for me. I know he wants to help me but I'm unsure if I want him trying to get into the castle. I'm also not sure I want to return to the castle in bat form, though. A wet fox in a tavern is less of a concern than a vampire in a castle. However, if Bianka is looking for me here, she's not in the castle.

That means if I'm going to rescue Lorelei, I need to hurry, because Bianka won't stay out here forever.

⮞

I leave my clothes by the barn and take to my bat form. Circling above the town, I see there are lights bobbing in the dark downstream from the mill. I can only hope Einhart can keep them busy for me. The ones by the mill aren't the only ones to worry about. In town I see three men carrying lanterns that give me the distinct impression of being police in plain clothes. They're trying to look non-descript, but the way they're carrying themselves seems like they're patrolling.

I don't bother circling them to figure out their intentions or where they're going beyond the fact they're not headed for the castle. I need to get there before word of my escape from Bianka reaches it.

The stones are unchanged from yesterday, but the clear weather gives me a sense of the scale I couldn't get in the fog. It really is a grand old citadel, and well preserved too. The ramparts are old and have not been converted to mount cannon on them. Against a modern army with artillery, it would not hold up well, but it certainly protected this area when it was built. The fact the castle is on a rocky outcrop also means an attacker would be more successful if they chose to shell the castle first, instead of attempting to breach the walls.

How I'm going to get Lorelei out of this place, I have no idea, but first I need to find her. She won't be in the archives, but she could be anywhere else in this castle.

This time, I decide to fly to the top of tower between the upper and lower ward, and I land there, changing back to myself. Walking along the rampart, I can see the entire complex. The lower ward seems to house the stables and barracks, while the upper ward has the main hall and the keep. It is quite possible this castle has extensive dungeons or a cistern that has been converted to a prison. It's also possible there is a cell built into one of the gatehouses. Honestly, Lorelei could be anywhere here.

I pace across the top of the tower, pondering where I should go. There is a lantern lit above the main gatehouse of the castle, and lanterns are in front of both entrances to the gatehouse between the wards. The keep is lit up, suggesting it's occupied, but the archive and other buildings are dark.

I growl, annoyed. Unless I can catch her scent, I'm not going to have an easy time of finding Lorelei. I transform back into a bat, and swoop down silently to the outer ward by the castle gate, landing in front of it as a fox. First, I pause to listen, and see if anyone noticed me. Then, I force myself to take in the scents of the surrounding area—actually concentrating on them. There's stone, the smell of the night air, and the scent of multiple people having passed this way.

Approaching the gate, I stay low, and carefully sniff. Since I've changed, my sense of smell isn't what it used to be, but that's because I no longer breathe. Forcing my unused lungs to push air in and out of my nose, I get a richer set of scents. There are the scents of a wolf, bear, and a lion, but no fox. I get down on all fours and actually sniff at the ground like my feral ancestors did to make sure.

I move around a little and sniff more, trying to pull the scents off the stone and mortar of the ground, but I can't tell.

Multiple paws seem to have passed this way recently, and it is difficult to get a read of what exactly happened.

I sit back on my haunches to think, tail draped across the cold ground. People seem to have headed toward the main gate, but also some seem to have headed toward what appears to be a stable. I opt not to search there, but I stand up and move over to the door of what I believe is a barracks.

Quickly scenting around there doesn't suggest anyone has been here today, so I move on. I spare myself the indignity of carefully searching the ground here since there aren't any fresh scents in this part of the ward. The fog from last night likely washed away any scents deposited from earlier than this morning.

At the inner gatehouse, there are a lot of different smells. I get down close to the ground, so I can take a moment to try and sort them out as best I can. Some of the smells seem similar to the outer gatehouse, but I think I catch the clear whiff of fox here.

I carefully proceed into the corridor connecting the two wards. It's not that long, and while it has a portcullis, it doesn't seem the gate here would hold during a siege as long as the outer gate would. Beyond the portcullis, at the end of the corridor, there seems to be a guardhouse, and at the door, the scent of fox becomes unmistakable. Not only that, it's not mine from being here last night.

I pause to listen. Again, there is silence, but I still try to open the heavy door carefully.

It resists my entry at first, but I'm able to get it open when I push a little harder. Unfortunately, that causes the door hinges to creak. They echo across the courtyard, and I can only hope there's no one here to notice.

Light from the lantern I used for a fire source last night bleeds inside. Carefully I pad in, and I leave the door ajar. This room inside is indeed a guard house. An ancient weapons rack rests against one wall, the wood darkened with age, waiting for swords and shields. The table inside appears just as old, but it's not dusty.

At the back there's a set of staircases, one leading down and another leading up. Forcing myself to once again breathe, I can sort the scents out here more easily. Lorelei seems to have passed through here, and not that long ago. Listening, I can hear someone that appears to be sleeping. Getting down again to sniff, the stone steps leading down seem promising, so I carefully descend those, trying not to let the claws on my footpaws click against the stone.

I expect there to be a large basement or dungeon, but it turns out there's a modest basement with a single cell at the back. In it, I can see the form of a fox on a stone bed. Her chest rises and falls slowly. A small lantern burns, hanging from a peg in the ceiling.

I don't need to force myself to smell to know this is Lorelei. She is fast asleep. There's also a problem I hadn't thought of. An iron cuff has been attached to one of her footpaws, and a chain runs to the wall in order to keep her secure. Even if I can get her cell open, I still need to get the cuff off.

The rest of the basement doesn't seem to have much. There's a table with some tin plates stacked on it. There's a wooden chest that has Lorelei's crossbow sitting on it, but nothing that seems to hold keys. Being turned has made me stronger, but there's no way I can break the iron chain or bend the jail cell's bars.

Creeping closer, I can see the lock looks old, but I've got no experience picking locks.

"Lorelei," I whisper, pressed against the bars. "Lorelei," I say again.

She rolls over. "What?" she says, half awake. One of her eyes is bruised.

"I need to get you out of here."

That rouses her and she sits up, blinking. "Radic?"

"Yes, come on. We need to go. Now where are the keys kept?"

She frowns, "I don't know. I think Bianka has them, but you shouldn't be here. You need to go."

My ears lay back. "Why does everyone keep telling me that?"

Her eyes narrow. "Who else told you that?"

"I met Einhart, the other vampire, and he told me I needed to leave too."

Lorelei gets up and comes to the bars. The chain drags across the stone. "Then go."

"I'm not leaving you."

"Radic, listen to me, take Ekrem and go. Get out of here as quickly as you can."

"Lorelei…"

"No! You need to go," she insists.

"Come on, there have to be keys here somewhere."

She sighs. "It doesn't matter if there were, I'd slow you down. The only way out is through the gate and they made sure I cannot leave. Go back to the house and get Ekrem. Take the journals and go. If I make it out, I'll find you in Vienna."

I flick my ears. "They're going to kill you, aren't they?"

She turns away from me. "Probably."

I reach out to touch her. "Lorelei, please…"

She looks back at me. "A feral animal in a trap will chew off its own paw to escape, but I will not give them the satisfaction of watching me do some form of that. In the end, I'm not what they want. They want you," she says.

"Why me though?"

"I should have seen it sooner, but I thought maybe Katarina didn't understand what was going on. In theory, the Huntsman could not die, but Mathias killed the Huntsman. He carried within him drops of the water of life, but a vampire has no need for eternal life, for they have eternal death. However, if you could purify the water of life from the blood of a vampire, you might too be able to experience eternal life as the Huntsman did."

"Does this even work?" I ask.

"I don't know, but Katarina killed Mathias before anyone could try it. He might have spawned others, but they would have even less of that essence then he did. Slowly rumors began to spread of a vampire who walked in the shadow of the night with more control. Who could hold their hunger at bay. Surely if any drops of the water of life were still within the bloodline of Mathias, this vampire would possess them."

I blink. "I fought hard to do that." I look down at my paws. "I killed and fed on people, Lorelei, way more than I have ever wanted to remember. You know what the journal says."

"I don't doubt you did. The curse seems far more powerful than any vestiges of the waters within you, but the Dragomirka hope to reclaim the birthright they feel the water of life gives them. Eternal life would let them rise to be emperor of the empire and who knows what else. You would be the only way to do that."

"This might not even work."

Lorelei sighs. "I know. I'm sure Bianka knows that, but they're determined. Katarina mentioned the theory in her journal, but it wasn't until they asked me point blank where you were that I realized someone actually believed this nonsense. This wouldn't be the first time they've sought out the water of life either. Whoever the signet ring belonged to likely did the same."

My mind races. "They know where your house is, right?"

"No, I told them I was staying in your room at the inn." If I had a heart that still beat, it would have stopped then. "I tried to buy you and Ekrem some time. I figured you and he deserve a chance to be happy." She stops when she sees my increasingly pained expression. "Ekrem … he didn't go back to the inn?"

I open my muzzle and can't get any words out at first. Finally, all I can get out is a pained croak. "Yes."

Hunters in the Night

Lorelei's ears fall and her whiskers droop at my response. She says "Go!" but I'm already heading for the stairs, taking them two at a time. I run through the guard room, fling open the outside door, and am running down the corridor between the castle's two wards with abandon before I transform into my bat form.

Ekrem … I need to get to Ekrem as fast as I can.

I beat my wings hard, pushing up and over the walls, barely clearing them. The air currents on the other side lift me up and I head straight toward the center of town, soaring high through the sky. My mind races, playing over scenarios about what is happening, but I can only fly so fast. As I descend from the castle, the houses rush by below me. Smoke rises from the chimneys, and I have to dodge left and right to fight the updrafts.

The town square looms ahead, and as I get closer, I can see a crowd by the inn. I want to land on one of the roofs to transform, but I don't know if I can stick the footing before I go sliding off the roof.

My heart sinks as I take in the scene. The three men I saw before are there, and between them is Ekrem. Bianka is also there, talking to Ekrem, and she gestures, but I have to fly by overhead before I can get a good look. As I bank hard to the left and circle overhead, I can see that Ekrem's hands are held behind him by one of the men, a lynx. Ekrem looks like he's been roughed up and had to be subdued. Even up above them, I catch a little blood scent in the air.

As I watch, they start walking, the lynx almost dragging Ekrem with him. It looks like they're taking him to the castle. I have no way of getting him and Lorelei out, and who knows what they'll do to him. There's nothing I can do.

Heartbroken, mind numb, I fly back to where I left my clothes next to a barn and transform back.

In the darkness, my mind races. Both Ekrem and Lorelei have been captured. I'm on my own again. I pick up the still wet clothes and slip my shirt on. It's cold against me, or at least I know it is supposed to be cold against me. Instead I feel nothing. I am nothing. I need to just run away, tail between my legs like I did a hundred years ago. There's nothing I can do but leave them. That's it.

I put my head against the side of the barn. But can I really leave them behind? Lorelei thinks I should leave, Einhart thinks I should leave, but can I leave? What the Dragomirka really need is me. I'm skeptical they can purify my blood, but they'll try. I know they'll try.

Katarina fought against this idea before, and apparently won, but she didn't stop it from coming back. As long as I'm alive, and someone knows who I am, they'll come looking for me.

All vampires are hunters, even myself, but the truth is all vampires end up being hunted. The only thing new in my existence is that I've tried to break the cycle as much as I can, and yet by not hunting, I've drawn the attention of a new kind of hunter: the nobility of the empire.

I slam my fist against the side of the barn in frustration. I have tried so hard to be left alone. I've tried so hard to control this curse. And yet the moment I find people who see beyond the curse, who know who I am, fate tries to rip them away from me.

I snarl and I can feel my canines lengthen as the curse inside me boils up. Well, I'm not running. Not this time.

I pull my shirt off and toss it back on the ground and return to my bat form. It's time I fight back. I can't leave them. I just can't do it. I hope they understand.

☙

As I fly toward the castle, my mind spins about what I can do. The simple answer is wait for everyone to go to sleep and then murder them all. Kill everyone, take the keys, and rescue Lorelei and Ekrem. I don't know how many there are, yet I do know that they haven't got enough men to man the ramparts. I could make the halls run red with blood.

But that's foolish. Bianka wants me to come to them. She's trying to lay traps, and if I give her time, she'll lay a trap with Ekrem and Lorelei. She has access to the day, where without darkness, I cannot survive. My only hope now is catching them off guard, when they're not expecting it.

As I approach the castle, I see the three men with Ekrem are heading toward the bridge to the gate. Once inside, they'll have the safety of the fortress, access to strong points and doors I cannot break down, and the familiarity of knowing what's in the castle. If I have any chance here, I need to use that sense of safety against them.

I circle above them, silently sizing them up, waiting for them to reach the bridge. Beyond the lynx, one is a badger, and the third, the leader of the group, is a stoat. Bianka isn't with them, so that's good. When the first one reaches the bridge, I dive down on the last one, the lynx, and let my form slip back to being a fox just before I reach him.

He doesn't hear me, but I've never tried something like this. I just get my paws out in front before I slam into him, using the lynx to break my fall. I flatten him into the stones, with a sickening crack.

"What the hell!" says the man in front of him, turning. The sudden appearance of a nude fox catches him off balance for a second. The badger is leading Ekrem, but he goes for a revolver of some kind under his jacket. I jump at him, and he steps aside, shoving Ekrem away from him. The only weapon I have is raw strength, so I throw myself at him. In the quick tussle the gun is knocked loose. Ekrem, for his part, stumbles and falls, his bound handpaws keeping him from catching his balance.

The stoat in front of me hesitates as I get clear of the badger, and while I take that as my moment to try and break his resolve and charge at him, he's quicker than I expect, pulling out not a gun, but a long knife.

He brandishes the blade, and I'm forced to block two quick slashes with my arms that slice them open. Next, he goes for a quick stab, and I step back, and the badger tries to grab me.

I growl, and throw my weight, trying to use the man holding me to disrupt my other assailant. The blade the stoat is wielding is long and thin, a fashionable weapon for quick deep stabs, and he knows how to use it. I feel another thrust slip by me as he aims for my stomach while I try and throw the badger off me.

There's a crack of a gun in my ear that causes us all to pause.

"Enough!"

I strain my neck to see who is behind me. There in the back is Bianka holding the pepperbox, walking up. She points the weapon straight at Ekrem.

"It's old, but it does the job well, I see," she remarks. "Now, if you don't want to see him dead, you'll stop this nonsense." She pulls back on the hammer to engage it.

The man around me has loosened his grip, but the stoat with the knife is still poised and ready. "Killing innocents I see," I remark.

She snorts. "It's your decision."

I feel my arms being tugged down, even though I'm bleeding onto my captors, but I resist. "You wouldn't."

She points the barrel directly at Ekrem's head. He whimpers, staring up at it. "Are you sure?" she says. "I have no sympathy for your kind, and that extends to those who associate with you."

She's going to do it. She's going to take his head off if I don't surrender. I can see the terrified look in his eyes.

"I…" I gulp. "I surrender."

She smiles and pulls the pepperbox back but keeps it pointed at Ekrem. "Put the handcuffs and collar on him, Jonatan," she says.

"Yes mam," says the stoat who produces the set of silver cuffs and begins to close them around me. When he's done, I feel cold metal being slipped around my neck and fastened shut. Satisfied that I'm secure, she walks up to me.

"I was worried you'd be hard to catch, but you're weak. I can see that now. You'd have been stronger if you fed well, but no matter. You're exactly who he wants." She glances up at the other two. The lynx I landed on has rolled over, but he looks pretty hurt. The badger is tending to him. "Take him to the village doctor, Filip, and get him bandaged up." She glances at the stoat, who is holding onto me. "Come on, we need to let Friderik know he can begin his preparations. We have his prize finally. Try to resist me at all, Radic, and Jonatan will kill Ekrem without a second's delay."

"Go to hell," I snarl, as she starts pulling me along.

"Not before I send you there first," says Bianka, with a curl in her muzzle. "Tonight, after all these years … is the night you will finally die."

∾

I am dragged into the castle and taken to the guard house of the inner gate. Jonatan gags me with a rag that tastes stale and old. I am left there chained to a post with Ekrem under guard by Jonatan. Bianka leaves for a few minutes. When she returns, she goes to fetch Lorelei from the cell downstairs.

Lorelei's ears fall when she sees me, but she tries not to let Bianka see. "Why am I here?" she asks.

The wolf gives her a glance. "You know why. You know who that is."

"Ekrem? Yes, I do. He lives in Strasek."

Bianka gives her a long, hard stare, her lips pulled back. "I don't know who the other fox is."

The wolf glances at me. "You've never met him?"

She shakes her head.

"That's Radic," Bianka says, giving her a hard stare.

Lorelei's ears flick back. "I've only seen him once, in the distance."

The wolf pulls back her lips to expose her fangs and gets up in Lorelei's face. "You're lying."

Lorelei regards her coolly. "And your proof is?"

Bianka's ears flick. "You're not one in a position, nor have the time, to play games."

Lorelei holds up her wrists, which are cuffed in front of her. "I've got all the time in the world right now, Bianka."

The wolf scoffs. "You think your sponsors in Vienna can protect you here?"

"I think they would be most interested in what deals you've made in Buda Castle far more than what I may or may not have done for a 'tame' vampire."

Bianka chuckles. "They would, but I'm not interested in the machinations of the Imperial court. The push and pull between Vienna and Budapest does not interest me."

"Then what are you interested in?" asks Lorelei. "Because I'd like to know what you think you're doing."

"Doing what I was paid to do. On that note," she turns toward me. "Whether you've met him or not doesn't matter. It's time you say goodbye."

Lorelei's ears flick back. "Bianka, no good can come of this," she says softly.

The wolf closes her eyes and takes a deep breath. "I don't need your condemnation." She glances towards Lorelei. "You had your chance to save him. Now, you will see his blood paint my blade."

The fox frowns. "What you're going to do may not work."

The wolf shrugs. "Faith is for the foolish."

Lorelei just looks confused, but there is a sound outside. The door to the guardhouse opens. A manservant, the lynx I saw before, quickly walks in. "His excellency, Friderik de Dragomirka," he announces. After him walks in a bear in a smoking jacket, a finely tailored shirt, and a pair of neatly pressed trousers. He has brown fur, a broad frame, and an eagerness about him.

Friderik takes one look at me and then wheels to Bianka. "You found him!" he says.

She gives a little curtsy. "As promised, your excellency."

The bear waves one of his paws. "This is no time for niceties. You are sure this is the one?"

"It is indeed," she says.

He turns toward me, and there's something in his eyes, something that I can describe almost as hunger. "Finally. I knew I could count on you, Bianka. You will be handsomely rewarded."

The wolf quirks up her muzzle at this.

"And the other one?" he says, pointing to Ekrem. He flicks his ears, but he doesn't say anything.

"He goes by the name of Ekrem. An accomplice I believe. He has the taint, but I do not believe he has been bitten."

The bear frowns. "Does he now?"

"Likely seduced."

Ekrem next to me scoffs at this, but Friderik doesn't seem to care. "Oh, I see. Hopefully we won't need him."

"I'm sure. I will have him and Lorelei held while you proceed with your research."

"Oh, my dear friend, the research was completed long before I was born." He walks over to me and eyes me like I'm a cut of meat in a butcher's shop. "The Dragomirka have searched for him for so long, we know what we must do." He frowns. He looks me up and down and finally seems to notice I'm naked. "Is there a reason he's nude?"

"He was attempting to rescue the leopard," responds Bianka. "He dropped down on the guards using his bat form."

"He got the jump on us, sir," says Jonatan. "Leon got hurt bad, but Bianka had anticipated the attack and hung back and interceded. Filip took Leon to the village doctor."

"Unfortunate, but it can't be helped." He turns away from me. "Come, let us perform this tonight and be done with it."

"Yes sir," says the stoat.

"Let me get the prisoners downstairs first," says Bianka, turning to lead Lorelei away.

A large paw falls on the wolf's shoulder. "Bring her to the lab. I will need her blood to help distill the essence. If the leopard is tainted too, I might need his also, but we'll start with the fox's. You can put the leopard in the cell."

The wolf's ears flick back and forth. "Only Radic has a connection to the Huntsman."

The bear turns away from her, and waves off her complaint. "I'm aware, but I need her also."

"Need me for what?" asks Lorelei.

Friderik de Dragomirka pauses and turns back toward her. "Radic's blood has the essence of the waters of life mixed with the curse of the vampire. Your blood has neither of those things, but you share some of his blood. To remove the essence from his blood, I will need to make a reactant from your blood, and the more related the better."

She blinks, and her lips draw back to expose her fangs. "I am not some chemistry experiment!"

The bear doesn't respond but just leaves the guardhouse, and I am pushed by Jonatan and the manservant out into the courtyard to follow him.

The Rites of Death

Gagged, handpaws bound behind me, I'm pushed across the inner courtyard of the castle toward the keep. Behind me, I can hear Lorelei struggling, cursing Bianka, but my mind is blank. This is it. Tonight, I will finally die again. They're going to bleed me like I bled so many people before. Judgment has come.

The entrance hall of the keep is a grand space of stone accented with polished wood behind two heavily reinforced doors. It's obviously been remodeled since the keep was built, since none of the defensive features I'd expect are here. I'm dragged across the parquet floor to a small door as Friderik heads for the main staircase at the back of the hall.

I can only gawk at the wealth displayed here; rich furnishings line the hall and tapestries hang from the walls. Moments later, I'm pushed through the open doorway. Behind it is a set of stone stairs, and I'm taken down a long flight of stairs with someone constantly pushing me onward until I reach the end. We then enter a large, pillared hall, and descend to the floor of the hall through a set of steps cut against the side of the wall. Light from various lanterns bounces around the space. This looks like it once served as a cistern, since the pillars have a visible water line on them, but it has long since been drained.

Simple stone sarcophagi have been laid out among the pillars, turning this into a crypt. I can feel the sense of death, but also a sense of belonging. The bones of the Dragomirka have been laid to rest here, and with them I feel at ease. They bring Lorelei and me to the center of the room and make us wait. I glance at her, but she is staring at her footpaws, ears and whiskers down, tail lifeless. The gag prevents me from speaking, but I want to say something to make it better, to make it at least right, but what would I say? What solace could I offer her right now? Nothing.

We wait in silence. I take this chance to look around. Off to one side, I can see a table has been set up as a workbench. Glass tubes and strange equipment are sitting on it. There are notes and an aged book along with a large glass pitcher containing an amber colored liquid. I have no clue what any of the lab equipment does.

A few minutes later Friderik enters. He has changed out of his smoking jacket into a simple shirt and a leather smock. It looks pristine, and yet I can tell this is his form of down dressing. He looks me over again, and smiles.

"Bring them over here in front of the great sarcophagus and secure them," he says, and I'm taken before the largest sarcophagus in the room. It has the words 'Our Beloved Elder' on the side of the stone slab. A chain is attacked to the collar around my neck, and then I am unceremoniously pulled down to a block and locked in place. I can hear scuffling as Lorelei is dragged in and secured also.

"Good, you may go and rest. I won't need you," he says to the guard and manservant. "Bianka will perform the cuts I need when I'm ready."

The wolf doesn't say anything at first. "On both?"

"Yes, on both. But first I must prepare. We cannot afford to let a drop of his blood go to waste, and who knows how much of hers we'll need. I will need at least an hour to prepare the reagents."

If the wolf responds, I don't catch it, and then I hear him walk off. A few moments later, I feel a presence over me, as she kneels down. I can glance up and just see her there.

"If I had my druthers about this, I'd kill you now and be done with it, but he's determined to reclaim his birthright."

I flick my ears back.

"I don't care what you have to say. You're a tainted creature, but," I feel her handpaw on top of my head, "even the damned deserve rest. I will see you are returned to your grave."

My ears go even further back. It's the only way I can express my disdain.

"I will not be swayed by that look. I know exactly what you are. There is no escape for you," she retorts.

I'm not sure if death, a real death, is what scares me more right now or that someone could believe the nonsense about vampires that Friderik does. There's nothing in the books I've seen, nothing in the myths, nothing in what Lorelei has told me that says you can use my blood for eternal life and not pay the cost I've paid. Only vague rumors suggest it's possible.

Bianka seems to understand that, because she leans down to whisper to me. "I said, you should have kept killing people. It would make you stronger, but you're weak."

I growl around the gag and try to pull myself up, testing my bindings.

"I'm afraid there's nothing you can do. I'll make sure the wound is clean and you bleed quickly. Then, I will have to bleed Lorelei, and I can be free of this cursed job." There's a pause. "Oh, and don't worry about him running around causing trouble as a vampire. If this alchemical nonsense doesn't work and he turns himself into a vampire, well, it's just another commission to collect. Might even do it for free with how he's treated me, but we'll see."

My eyes get wide, and she gets up. "I can't leave a mess behind, after all." She steps away outside of my vision, and I hear a sigh and movement. There is the clatter of a chain and then the words, "I'm sorry, Lorelei."

The low growl held in the back of a throat is clear.

"Yes, well, I know. It's not how I wanted this to end."

The growl turns lower, and even if it is muffled it is murderous.

"Well, you should have done what your sponsors in Vienna wanted you to do."

There's a rattle of chains, but no response from Bianka, only the sound of claws against the stone fading away. I'm left there, on the ground. I strain to turn my neck against the collar and can just see Lorelei's face, with her ears back, now also gagged like I am. It looks like she's crying.

There's nothing I can do here. I can't save her. I can't save myself. There is nothing left to do but wait, so I wait, chained to the floor before the sarcophagus. I hear Friderik working at preparing for the extraction of my blood, but I let myself go. I just am, no longer aware. It might be only minutes; it might be an hour or two. I don't know. There's nothing more to say. I lived a short life, and a much longer undeath, but I don't know what lies on the other side. I have tried to make right my many wrongs, so in that, I am at least at peace with myself. I worked to be more than the curse wanted me to be. I just wish that Lorelei didn't need to pay the price for my crimes.

Eventually, the scraping of a claw against the stone nearby catches my attention, and I feel the touch of a paw on my back. My time must be up, and the reagents must be ready. Bianka doesn't say anything, and I just keep my eyes closed. This is it. This is my true death.

I feel something against my back and the sound of something fumbling. Then there is a click.

My eyes shoot open as the chains start to loosen.

"We need to hurry, Radic"

Ekrem? The chain holding my arms slips away, and as I pull myself up with his assistance. Next to Lorelei, Einhart is trying to unchain her.

I scramble to shake off my bindings, and I reach up to undo the gag tied to my head.

"We need to go," Einhart whispers, as he gets Lorelei's bindings undone.

I can run, I can flee, but what good does that do me? But first, "How are you here?"

"Einhart killed the only guard in the guardhouse and let me out," Ekrem says, pointing to the weasel as he's getting Lorelei up. "We don't have much time."

"No," I say. "They'll follow. Take Lorelei and get away. I need to stop this from happening."

"This is a cursed place," growls Einhart. "This is where the pain begins. Do you want to know the pain?" he asks me.

"No, but they'll pursue me, and Lorelei," I say, then glance around. "Where are the other guards?"

"I don't know. I saw Friderik leave to get something, and I took this chance. Come!" he says, heading for the stairs.

"He won't be long," responds Lorelei, also heading for the entrance.

I glance toward the table with the alchemical equipment. Among the glassware and jars containing various chemicals, sitting on top of scattered papers, is a book. It looks old, and whatever secrets he's uncovered that I don't know about, they're likely in it. If it tells Friderik how to distill my blood, it might tell me how to cure my condition and Einhart's.

"She's right, we need to go, Radic," says Ekrem. He stops when he notices I'm not coming. "Radic?"

I go to the table and pick up the book. The cover is old, the leather worn, but if there's a cure, it could be in here. Next it to are notes with symbols scratched on them and I grab them all from the table.

"I can't leave this here," I say, turning away from the table as I shove the loose sheets of paper into the leather book. "Whatever Frederik found this is likely it. It's too dangerous to leave with him."

Ekrem nods, and I follow them toward the stairs where Einhart waits, listening. "I don't know where the other guards are," he whispers, "I know Friderik went upstairs, but I did not see Bianka."

"That could be a problem," I say.

"Only if they want to die," he says with a little laugh.

I notice Einhart offers no qualification of who he means, because he means this about all of them. He did not need to be invited in to the castle, because he's been here before. It likely wasn't willingly either. His use to Friderik and Bianka is over, so there won't be any mercy for him.

"Let me go first. All of you are here because of me."

Einhart nods, and Lorelei speaks up. "Let me take the book then."

I hand it over and then start up the stairs.

Reaching the main floor, I pause by the doorway and look out into the hall. Two iron wheel chandeliers hanging in the room, lit with candles, light up the hall. The tapestries I noticed earlier seem to depict various events in history connected to the castle, but there are also many paintings of bears. I'm sure one of these depicts the story of the Huntsman. In the back of the room, there is a grand staircase, leading up.

"Quickly, toward the ga—" I say, stepping forward, heading toward the main door. There is a twang sound, and my voice is cut short. I fall to my knees. Pain explodes across my body.

It takes me a moment, but I touch my stomach. There is a hole in it now, and my paw comes away wet.

There is blood.

My blood. There's a lot of it, and I feel myself slip to the ground.

"You're not as clever as you think, Einhart."

I blink and turn my head. Bianka is there, having emerged from through a different doorway, holding her crossbow in one arm, but she's got the pepperbox up and pointed toward us.

"Damn you to hell," growls Lorelei.

"That will be for God to judge me, not you."

The weasel's nose flares, but he stands his ground. "You can't do this. He'll hunt us all, even you, if you give him this power."

She laughs. "Spare me your tears." She takes careful aim with the pepperbox. "I'm sorry your family will have to suffer for this, but you don't."

Lying on the ground, I can do nothing as I watch. Bianka fires first at Einhart, striking the weasel in the arm, as he starts to transform. There's a sickening shriek, as he hits the ground as a bat. Lorelei and Ekrem charge her, and she wheels the gun around and fires twice. I can see she grazes Lorelei and then puts a ball right through Ekrem.

The leopard falls to the parquet wooden floor just like me, as Lorelei slams into Bianka and the pepperbox goes flying and skids across the entrance hall. I hear cursing, but all I can focus on is Ekrem, lying on the ground.

His back is turned to me, and his breathing is ragged. He's going to die from this. I realize with horror that I will live, or at least live long enough until I can serve Friderik's goals. He'll make sure I'm kept alive until he can make whatever weird potion from my blood he desires.

I close my eyes. There's the sound of struggle, a scream, shouting, and another shot going off. But I lie waiting to be collected. It's a debilitating wound, but not a fatal one. Lorelei knew what to do.

"Vessel of my blood…"

I look up. There's a bear I've never seen standing over me.

"Vessel of my blood, arise."

He's big. There's a ragged scar across his throat where it has been cut, and yet he still speaks. He kneels down and I feel a paw under my muzzle. "You must get up."

The edge of his form seems almost translucent, like the tips of his fur are not quite here. There's something incorporeal about him, but in my dazed state I cannot understand why that is.

"Is not my death enough?" I croak.

The bear shakes his head. I can see he wears clothes very out of style with a dark green sash around his waist. He looks at me sadly. "Your strength was my strength. You must finish the hunt, for I cannot."

Shakily, I push myself up. Part of my stomach is missing, and yet, I feel no pain now. I feel only sadness.

The bear looks toward the stairs, "He is coming back. Kill him."

"What?" I ask in surprise, but the figure is gone then.

Swiveling my head, I can see Lorelei standing over Bianka with the pepperbox in her handpaw. A trickle of blood drips out of the wolf's muzzle, and her tail is still upon the ground. There are frantic footsteps on the grand stairs.

"We need to go," says Lorelei.

"Not yet," I say striding over to pick up the crossbow where it has fallen. There's no time to load it, but my eyes are on Friderik who is at the top of the stairs. "This ends tonight," I growl.

"No! You should still be downstairs," says the bear, coming down. He reaches into his coat pocket to pull something out, but I don't give him a chance to retrieve it. I rush forward and swing with the crossbow as he reaches the bottom of the stairs.

The crunch is sickening, and I see him fall to the ground stunned. There is blood, and my fangs ache. I am hungry. I haven't fed recently, and the only way to heal quickly is fresh blood. I shouldn't let a good meal go to waste, but I know what I need to.

I kneel down looking at the dazed bear. There's movement behind me, but I don't turn. "You know, as much as you want my blood, I don't want yours," I remark, handpaws wrapping around his neck.

"No…" he gags.

I close my eyes. "May you find peace," I whisper, and then I squeeze.

He kicks, and as he does I hear Lorelei say something, but it doesn't register. I wait, paws wrapped around his neck. The meal he would make for me would not be taken without reason, and yet, I just hold with all my strength, waiting.

The body goes limp, but I wait longer, ten, fifteen seconds.

"You know, I could just shoot him for you."

I let go and look up. "It had to be me." I know in that moment that this is what the Huntsman wanted.

Lorelei holds out a handpaw and pulls me upright. She's got the pepperbox in the other one.

"Ekrem…" I say.

She points, and I hurry over. Ekrem is still lying on his side, and I kneel next to him. He's breathing, but just barely.

"We need to get you out of here," I whisper, scooping him into my arms. He moans. "Do you think anyone heard the gunshots?" I ask absently, holding him to me.

"Maybe," says Lorelei. "There have to be servants here, but I don't know how many guards are here. The two that went to the doctor may not be back yet."

"Let them come, my fangs are hungry." I glance up, and I see Einhart has returned to his weasel form. He's been hit in the shoulder, and one arm hangs broken and useless. He wavers but reaches the grand doors to use them to brace himself. I don't know who else is here, but there is only one priority for me right now.

"Hey, it's going to be okay," I say to Ekrem softly.

He groans. "Radic…"

"We'll get you a doctor."

"It's…" he coughs wetly, "not going to matter."

"Ekrem?" I pull him even tighter to me. He feels wet. Oh god, he's covered in so much blood. The fur is matted, and holding him, I can feel the raw flesh where the bullet passed through his chest.

"Sorry…" he mumbles.

"No, you…" my voice breaks, and I listen to his ragged breathing. I think the bullet went through his lungs, or at least nicked one. His heart sounds so weak. He's fading.

"Radic…" his paw weakly grips me. "Drink."

I feel everything stop. My mind frozen.

"Dri … nk."

"I can't," I cough out. "I won't."

His pulse is slowing. "Please…"

My body shivers. There's no time to think this through. I told myself I would never do this again. Why is he asking me to do this? "Ekrem…"

I feel him slipping away as his body is giving out on him.

"I'm sorry," I say, and then I reach toward his neck. My fangs slide out freely. I never wanted to do this again, not to a talking, thinking creature.

His eyes look at me in an unfocused way, and then, with the last of his strength, the leopard bares his neck.

The Embrace of Eternity

The taste is divine, just like the first time I killed a sapient creature. Ekrem shivers in my embrace. He very weakly pushes back against me, but his eyes quickly roll back. He's already suffered a lot of blood loss. There's not much life left in him, but before he gasps a final time, I pass over a drop of my essence.

I bite my own arm and then lower it to his lips. "Drink."

Feebly, he licks at my arm, and then I bend down to finish my meal.

When he goes slack and there's nothing left to take, I release my hold and lick my fangs. Then I gently lay him down and cross his arms in repose. I sit back on my haunches and just look at him, letting this moment sink in. I've done it. I've finally made another of my kind.

The leopard is dead, and I'm covered in his blood and my own blood.

The color has drained from his lips, and the muscles have all gone slack. His eyes are glassy. I can no longer hear his heartbeat, and I will never hear it again.

I, in the meantime, have not felt this alive in a long time. Power courses through me in a way I had forgotten it could. I feel like a god right now.

"You … turned him…" I can hear Lorelei.

I turn toward the fox, still crouched down, and wipe the blood from my mouth, onto the back of my paw, even though I'm covered in blood. "Yes."

She looks at me and then over to Einhart, unsure and confused. Einhart is cradling the arm that was shot. That doesn't mean he's not still dangerous. The only thing she has to protect herself from us right now is the pepperbox.

"You think I shouldn't have?" I say, standing up. I can feel power inside myself. I could take her too. It would be easy right now, and oh has it been so long since I've had a meal like this. So so long…

"I…" She has the gun in her paws, but it's not pointed at me.

I am power now. My senses are sharpened, and even with the gaping wound in my stomach, I feel strength inside of myself I haven't felt in so long. Lorelei's ears flick, concerned, and I wrap my will around her then. She's vulnerable, unsure of what to do, and with that, I can bend her.

I pull at her, pulling in a way I haven't in so long. "Give me the pepperbox," I command.

She hesitates, confused, then obediently she holds it out. I walk over and take it. Afterward, she blinks at me, and realization dawns on what I just did. "You have a strong will," I say, looking over the weapon in my paws.

So much power in my paws now. So much strength, and yet so fleeting it is.

"You just—" she stammers.

"Yes." Her heart beats faster. "You have a strong sense of self, and yet in a moment of confusion, I pushed." I look at the gun, and I feel my paws shake. "It's so easy right now."

"I did not rescue you for you to just fall for temptation," rasps Einhart. "You need to find composure."

What have I become? "Ninety years wasted," I whisper.

Lorelei growls. "Give me the gun back."

Weakly I hold it up, and she snatches it back.

"I'm still the monster," I whisper, my mind now in turmoil. Inside myself, I feel the pain of my own death, the fear and the horror I became, and the loss of my own self. The war of my will against my own body has never gone away. I have spent a century in turmoil and yet even after all that, I slipped right back into it.

Worst of all, I'm still hungry.

"We should go," remarks Einhart.

I fix my eyes on my great-grandniece. She looks scared. Her ears are back, and her tail is curled against her, but beyond her fear, I can tell there is sadness. "Lorelei, I'm sorry," I whisper. "It only works in moments of uncertainty in the one who is influenced, and your will is strong."

Her eyes are like saucers. She's scared. I could do it again. I could break her in this moment because deep down she cares. She cares about me, and that is her weakness. That is where she lets me push against her. To prey on those who love you is the true horror of this curse, because those are always the easiest ones. They are the most vulnerable.

She blinks, and I turn toward Einhart. "You're right," I say. In this moment, I must find my strength and my resolve. I must not succumb to myself. "We need to go."

The darkness inside me spirals ever lower, and yet at the bottom, at the very bottom of myself, there is hope. Hope for myself and hope to be more than just the monster. Is it enough to keep the urges at bay still? I don't know, but I must still put myself above the horror.

"Right, who knows what other guards there are. There have to be servants," says Lorelei. She starts picking up the dropped notes, and that's good. I haven't pushed her too far.

I just need to let the blood high pass and she'll be beyond me again.

"Of course." I glance toward the back of the hall. "We need to—"

I freeze. The portrait in the back of the room over the stairs.

"Radic?"

Lorelei, Ekrem, and I are not the only hunters here.

"Radic!"

The portrait is old. It shows a lord standing before his keep, but I've seen that bear before and the green sash around his waist.

"Radic!" Einhart snaps his fingers at me. "We're leaving."

"Not yet. He's here," I say, and I feel it then. Family, but not my blood family; the family that I carry now because I carry the water of life inside of me. The family I never wanted. This was his home before it was Friderik's, back when it was just a keep and not much more. The picture is almost smiling. Why is he smiling?

Well, if he's here, that means I can call to him.

"Giver of my twisted blood, arise!" I intone, stepping toward the stairs, focusing on the picture.

There's nothing.

"Are you okay?" asks Lorelei.

I shake my head. "I thought—"

"The deed is done. You may leave," booms a voice.

Three sets of hackles go up. Where in the middle of hall there was no one, now stands a bear who is not quite there. "The Huntsman," whispers Lorelei.

Indeed, it is. "Why did you have me kill Friderik?" I ask.

The spirit bear gives a soft chuckle. "If I had wanted my children to be possessed by my gifts, I'd have shared it with them. Instead, I alone took the burden upon myself, for the gifts came at the cost of slipping out of time, just like you have slipped out of your own time."

"If I could give you the essence of the water of life back, I would," I say.

The Huntsman snorts. "And I would refuse it."

I understand in the moment what he has suffered, not in darkness like I have, but in isolation through centuries bound to a duty he could never give up. Only when it was ripped away from him did any peace come.

"Then what happens now?" I ask.

The bear turns away from me. "Leave. My descendants will find their way," he says, and slowly he fades from view.

I stare at the emptiness, until I feel Lorelei's paw on my shoulder. "Come on."

My ears go back. The picture frame at the back of the hall has returned to a more regal stance. There is no smirk anymore but a somber expression. "I want answers."

"Not everything in life gives answers," remarks Einhart. "Why did Friderik do those experiments to me? Why does it still hurt? Why can I still hear my own screams in my sleep?" The weasel stops and shakes his head. "There will never be answers. There will never be an apology. All I can do is hope the scars heal."

I glance toward the body of Friderik. Part of why he did what he did to Einhart might be in the notes, but there will be no apology. To him, we were all just tools.

I flex my handpaw, feeling the blunted claws. I've spent so long trying not to be the killer. I've spent so long not wanting to be the monster, yet that is all I am to the Dragomirka. Worse, like the monster I've tried not to be, I've taken two lives tonight. Lorelei took one herself, and I tempted my fate in ways I have not in a long time. All of this because of the man who now lies dead at the bottom of the stairs.

I squeeze my paw shut. I won't let others and the curse decide who I am. I will.

"You're right, let's go," I say, walking over to where Ekrem lies. I kneel and scoop the leopard up into my arms and easily lift him. Since I've just fed, it's almost like he weighs nothing in my arms. Einhart cracks open the door and looks outside, and then we set off, with Lorelei following behind me after she picks up the book and papers she dropped fighting Bianka.

Out in the courtyard, the night is cool, and the stars are bright with possibilities that are far beyond my grasp. Only in my bat form can I touch them, and so fleeting they always are.

"Where are the guards?" whispers Lorelei.

"I don't know, but I took care of two people," says Einhart.

"Two went to the village doctor," I say, trying to keep my voice down, as I follow Einhart across the inner castle ward. The smell of death hits me before we reach the passage between the wards. In the dark of the entranceway, I can see the manservant I saw who helped bring Lorelei and I downstairs earlier. He's been drained.

"Not exactly discreet," I say.

The weasel glances toward me. "I had to think fast. There was no reason to let the meal go to waste."

"Yes, but…" I falter. Who am I to judge right now?

Einhart pauses in the corridor. "We will always be what we are. Accepting it is how you find peace."

I'm silent for a moment, and then I speak up. "I want to be better."

He chuckles. "Just because you don't drink the blood of the sapient creatures that talk does not change who you are. You are no better than I because you don't drink blood like I do, and tonight we are both the same."

"I know, but I don't want to be the monster. Not if I don't have to be."

"You fought it, I accepted it. Look how easy it was for you to slip back into it after you drained Ekrem."

"Do you miss the sun? The warmth of life inside yourself?" I ask.

He stops to laugh. "Ah, but I have warmth again." He turns towards me. "It came at a cost."

"What did they do to you?" I ask.

"Experiments, injections, I wasn't always conscious for what Friderik did to me. Sometimes days would pass, and I'd wake up bound with him muttering over his work table. I don't know what he hoped to achieve, but whatever it is didn't work as he thought it would. I changed, but not in the way he expected."

"You two are the worst at stealth," hisses Lorelei.

I'd ask more questions but she's right, and we both fall silent and then continue down the corridor to the outer ward. It appears deserted, and the castle gate is open. Einhart glances around and then pads across the courtyard, crouching down low, sniffing. I follow the weasel, still carrying Ekrem in my arms. Lorelei trails us, the pepperbox at rest, but ready to take aim.

Near the gate Einhart pauses and gets close to the wall. I'm coming up behind him with Ekrem when I hear something.

"Voices," I whisper, as my tail tenses up. We're in the courtyard, and whoever is coming is entering the castle.

Einhart glances. "I can take them," he says, crouching down, favoring his wounded arm.

I hear the sound of a door opening behind me. "Or we just hide," whispers Lorelei.

There's no point arguing and I quickly follow Lorelei into the gatehouse for the main gate. Einhart glances back, hesitates, and then follows. Carefully she closes the door. It's a good hiding place, but I'm covered in blood and Einhart is hurt. There's no way they won't notice us.

We wait, and finally I can catch words.

"I just have a feeling that whatever he's doing could be really bad," says a voice. I think it's the badger from earlier. "That fox is dangerous."

I hear a strained cough and the clunk of wood against the flagstones. "Like any of this isn't trouble."

"I know, but the baron will do what he wishes." There is a pause and the sound of claws against the stone stops. "I think I smell blood."

There's a sniff. "I do too."

I hear fabric moving and a click of something metallic. I think it's the sound of a hammer being drawn on a gun. "Do you think we should investigate?"

"I'm in no condition to tangle with that fox if he's loose, Filip."

There's more sniffing. "Something has happened."

"Filip, do you have any idea how to fight a vampire?"

"Not a clue." There's a pause. "Do bullets work?"

"I think so. You want to go and look?"

There's a sigh. "No, but I will. First though, let me get you back to the barracks."

We hear them shuffle off, and through the gap in the door, I can see them head towards the barracks on the other side of the ward, but holding Ekrem, I can't really get a good view. Lorelei watches carefully and when it's safe, she motions for us to move. Quickly we exit the gatehouse, then go through the tunnel and across the bridge.

"I think we're free," says Lorelei.

"Good. It's best we part ways here," says Einhart. "I'll wait here for a bit, and if someone follows you, I'll create a distraction."

"You probably can't fly with the state of your arm," says Lorelei.

Einhart shrugs. "I know, but you need to get away."

"I appreciate it," remarks Lorelei, "but the nudity will draw the attention of anyone who comes by."

"Clothing or not, I don't think it will matter to Friderik's men."

I nod. "Where will you go after tonight?"

"I need to go to Kraków first, to take care of some things, but then I will come to Vienna. You've given me much to think about, Radic. Perhaps there is a way to find a better path for me, like you found it."

I want to ask what he needs to take care of, but I gather it entails something to do with his own relatives. "Then safe travels."

"Indeed, journey safe," adds Lorelei. I can tell she feels hesitant about that, and I understand. She's letting her prey escape.

"You too," Einhart says. "Keep Ekrem safe."

"I will," I say, and we set off through the town.

࿇

I thought I might have to explain to someone in the village why I'm nude, covered in blood, and carrying a lifeless body through town, but the night is quiet with how late it is. We don't talk, and that's probably for the best. We see no one on the walk back to the farmhouse. There is no one there waiting for us either.

Halfway back, I can tell the blood high from having fed is starting to fade. The hole in my stomach has started to finally hurt again, and Ekrem no longer feels feather-light in my arms. Still, I get him back with no difficulty at all.

Lorelei goes into the house, and I take Ekrem down into the root cellar to lay him down. Before going inside, I go to the well and pump up some water so I can wash the gore out of my fur. My stomach hurts more and more. While I know it will heal rather quickly, I've still got a hole in me that's oozing blood. Dawn can't be far away, but I'd like to talk to Lorelei.

Upon entering, I find her sitting at the table with just a lantern burning. There's an open bottle of wine, but no glass. The book and the notes are pushed to one side, along with the pepperbox.

"Do you have a bandage?" I ask.

She points to a dresser on one side of the room, and I go over to it. Carefully I bind my wound. When I'm done, I notice Lorelei hasn't really moved. She's staring off into space.

"You know, I had made a fire just after dark, to welcome you and Ekrem back home. I was even thinking of attempting to make dinner for you, but I wasn't sure I could pull that off," I say.

"Such a simpler time last night was," she says, as she reaches for the bottle. She takes a sip. When she's done, she leans back to consider me.

"Are you afraid?" I say, sitting down in a chair across from her.

Her ears fall back. "Afraid?"

"Yes."

"Of you?"

"Of that or the Dragomirka."

She frowns. "There's still one chamber in the pepperbox that's loaded."

"I understand if you think you need to use it."

She lowers her muzzle. "Do you now?"

I hold my handpaws so I can look at them. "No matter what I do, what is in my veins is valuable to someone else."

"Just like what is in my veins is valuable to you."

I squeeze my handpaws shut and look down. "Lorelei … I couldn't let him go. He asked. No one ever asked."

"What if Friderik had asked?"

I look up. "People like him don't ask."

"Yes, but what if one of the Dragomirka does ask. What if I asked?"

I consider only briefly. "You're family, they're not. I'd do it, if you asked, but think long and hard on that."

She doesn't say anything after that for a while.

"Well, it's true," I offer.

"You do realize I've killed vampires before, correct?"

"Yes."

"I need to know I can trust you, Radic. What you've done tonight does not end the threat of the Dragomirka. If they catch word of you again, they will pursue. It's not just you either now. Blood relation or not, I cannot have you or Ekrem preying on innocents."

I frown. "I will teach Ekrem what I've learned about the hunger." My ears flick. "If he turns. I don't know how much of my blood it takes."

She is silent for a moment. "Emotions aside, you could have let him go."

"I…" I swallow, trying not to sound like I'm convincing myself instead of her. "I did it because he asked. There wasn't time to argue."

"Yes, but you, of all people, should know what the cost of eternal life is," insists Lorelei.

"I do. I'm not sure he does, but he'll learn." I pause to consider. "What about Einhart?"

She sighs. "If he continues to be a problem, someone will come for him. You are still in danger, no matter what you do now."

I look over one of my paws and the black fur on it. "The essence is still within me, and some of it must be in Ekrem now."

"Yes, and you must tread carefully."

"I'm sorry also about the push. It's been so long since I've done that to someone."

She doesn't say anything, but her eyes fall to the pepperbox. "Am I prey for you?"

"No! Never." I growl and slam my fist down. "I will not let this curse consume me. I will not yield to it again."

Her ears droop. "We both know the hunger will always be there."

I lean back in the chair and stare up at the ceiling. "Yes, it is. No matter what, it always is there." I sigh. "Why is it so much harder to not be the monster than to just be the monster?"

That does give her something to consider and I see her whiskers twitch before she responds. "Monsters are easy to understand. They're just bad, and monsters get hunted. To be what you work to be is to be something else."

I drum my claws on the table and then focus my gaze back to Lorelei. "What about you? Can I trust you not to turn me in?"

Her ears perk. "That's a good question. There are those I wish I could tell about you, but they're all gone. If I die, only the Dragomirka and Einhart know the truth of tonight."

"And?" I ask, leaning forward.

She takes a long drink from the wine bottle. "I will have to be careful when I return to Vienna. Hopefully my patron doesn't ask too many questions."

This makes my ear perk. "Who is your patron?"

"A minor lady, but she has the ear of the archduke."

I feel my hackles go up. "Lorelei…"

She raises one of her handpaws to cut me off. "I doubt the Dragomirka will want to let it slip what they're after. That would be of great interest to the archduke and the emperor himself. In this game, I am not important to them, Radic. You are."

"This should be over."

She shrugs. "Only if we're lucky. Wealth combined with your powers is a seductive and dangerous combination, but that doesn't mean anyone else knows what Friderik did."

I sit back. "I know. I never asked for this attention."

"One never does," she takes a sip of the wine, and sets the bottle down. "But one must know who they really are. For your safety, it would be better if we never talked again after tonight."

I feel that like a knife across my heart. "I … don't want to lose you. Not like I lost Katarina."

"Radic, you know we shouldn't. Not if you and Ekrem are going to be safe."

I growl. "No. We are family. I cannot let them take you away from me."

"Time will do that anyway."

I sigh and look down. "I know, but not yet. I have no desire to hurry the inevitable."

"I can't know where you are. If someone finds out I do, it will be disastrous. I already have to lie about why I'm not still locked up in a castle, prisoner of a dead baron."

I reach for her free handpaw, the one not resting on the bottle of wine, taking it into mine. "You never found where I was in Vienna."

She looks at my paws wrapped around her. "Radic…"

I steel myself. "Please. I can't go back into the shadows like that, even with Ekrem. I need to find something to keep myself feeling alive. I need people to care about."

She searches my face in the light from the lantern. "I understand, but it will be dangerous for both of us."

"Yes, it will be, but is to be happy too much to ask of this world?"

"No, no it is not." She swirls the contents of the bottle of wine. "You want some wine?"

"Yes, just a bit. I don't want to be sick."

She tilts the bottle toward me. "Then to family and to hope."

I take the bottle and take a big gulp of wine. It's a red, and the taste is dark and rich. I then offer the bottle to Lorelei who takes a drink herself. "To family and hope," I reply.

She nods and then yawns, tongue rolling out of her muzzle. "I need to get some sleep."

"Of course," I respond. "Do you mind if I look over the book and notes before I go to bed?"

"Be my guest," she says.

❧

After everything that happened, you'd think I would be tired, but I'm not. I'm too wound up to rest, and the blood high from having fed has me feeling jittery, even though my stomach aches from the arrow wound. Lorelei goes to bed, but first I make sure to clean up Ekrem. Then, I take a lantern, a clean sheet, and the notes to the root cellar to join him. The leopard doesn't stir, but I don't expect him to.

I gently kiss his forehead, and start going over what we took from the castle. A few hours later though, after the sun has come up, I realize I'm getting nowhere. The book and the notes from Friderik are useless. The book turns out to be a copy of an alchemy book from 1627. It's interesting, but I can't tell if any of it is right. I can't tell how to test any of this. Some of the things the book suggests seem like complete nonsense. As for Friderik's notes, they're disheveled, and they don't tell me a lot.

It appears the Dragomirka previously devised a reagent of some kind; this must be what he said was researched before he was born. I can see what Friderik planned to do chemically with it, but how he knows it works is not here. That must be in some journal he kept, or this is what was passed down to him.

At this point, I have nothing else to go on if there is a cure for my condition. There's no way to stop it and no way to reverse it. I just exist, and that's it. There's nothing more to it, and there's nothing more I can do unless I want to go back to the castle and start ransacking Friderik's rooms. I just don't have the understanding of chemistry to judge the merit of Friderik's work, but since some of it appears to have come from the alchemy book, it very well could be the delusions of someone who dreams of power. It's possible I'm missing something, but I have a hunch that going over the book and notes carefully won't help me. There's a piece to this puzzle still missing.

It's not till well after dawn that I finally put the book and notes down on the sheet, and I curl up on the other side of the root cellar from where I laid Ekrem. I blow out the lantern, and lie back to just think, trying to make sense of the formulas and alchemical symbols I don't understand. My mind drifts, and it's only then that I sleep because the next thing I know is I can hear my name.

"Radic?"

I'm bolted awake with a silent gasp. "Yes?" I ask cautiously, as light filters down into the root cellar. I look up and see Lorelei at the entrance holding a lantern. Night has fallen already.

"Are you getting up?"

"How late is it?" I inquire.

"An hour past sunset."

"Normally, I synchronize with the sun, but I guess staying up to read will undo that," I remark, getting up and picking up the books.

She nods and waits for me to come up. "Did you find anything useful in those?"

"No. I will take my time to decipher it, but I somehow doubt there's anything in there about a cure. Friderik also relied on research his ancestors conducted, which isn't here."

"Well, it's something to pursue." She pauses. "I need to return to Vienna."

My ears droop. "Already?"

"I've given it some thought, and I considered what you said. For now, it's best I sneak away before someone realizes I'm not in the castle's dungeon."

"Did you go into town?"

She nods. "I did but not to Tarcsa. I went to Strasek instead. I arranged for your trunk to be brought here tomorrow. I included some of Ekrem's things in it. I will leave tonight."

"Did they ask why?"

"No, but word of my capture already reached them. I told them it was a misunderstanding."

I feel my ears and tail droop. "So, this is it."

"For the moment. I assume you'll follow once you're ready."

"Yes, but if you're not here, I can't just stay in a root cellar."

"That I have also given thought to. There's a cave a few miles from here up on the foothills that seems to be clean and deserted. I checked it out when I was looking for you and Einhart. I think it would give you a place to hide. It shouldn't be too hard to drag your trunk over there. I'll give you the address of who I have bringing it. They should be able to forward it to Vienna for you when you're ready. They're going to send mine to Vienna."

I ponder. "This is useful, but will it be wise to do that?"

"Maybe not, but I helped the people in Strasek out with what happened to Alina. That means more than what happened in Tarcsa. News of Friderik's death doesn't seem to have escaped the castle yet."

I frown. "It's unsettling to think he might not be dead, but I felt him go limp around me with my own handpaws."

"If Friderik is not dead, then neither of us want to be anywhere near here."

I shudder. "Agreed, but even so, there's also the rest of the family to contend with. Will you be safe in Vienna?"

"I should be, and I have the ear of Eleonore, Countess of Wolfurt, if need be. She is my patron."

I rack my brain, trying to think if I've ever heard of the title, but nothing comes up. "I'm not familiar with Wolfurt."

"It's small, and not really important, but she is well respected at court, even with the recent reorganization of imperial affairs," she says.

"I'm sure the Dragomirka have their allies in Buda Castle, and recent reforms have probably given them leverage beyond the court in Vienna."

"Of course, but in Vienna, they cannot operate directly, at least not away from the eyes of the imperial court." She shakes her head. "All of this assumes of course that they know you'll be in Vienna."

"It's a fair assumption, but discretion has always been how I survived. On that, where is the cave?"

"North, close to where the mountains start to rise. I can show you."

"No, just tell me where, and I'll find it. It's best we do part ways while there's time."

Lorelei nods and tells me how to find the cave. I listen carefully and she draws me a simple map of where it is. It should be easy to find in my bat form, and I'll move Ekrem there once I know for sure where it is. It's much closer than the one to the west I used as my waypoint on the way to Strasek.

"Will you be okay?" she asks once we're done, and she's gathered her traveling things into a backpack.

"I believe so," I say, fidgeting by picking at the fur at my elbow. "We will follow as soon as we can."

"Be safe," she says.

"The same goes for you," I respond.

We lapse into silence.

"I should go now," she says, turning away from me. "With luck, I can reach Ungvar in two days and catch a train there."

I reach out and gently take her handpaw, and she turns back to me, as I wrap my arms around Lorelei. I'm just a little taller than her. "Thank you," I say. "You didn't have to let me live."

She hugs me back. "It's okay. You deserve better than what happened. Katarina would agree."

There's something I have to say to her. "Also, even though I've already apologized, I'm sorry that I made you give me the gun last night. In that moment I thought you might do something rash, but I also shouldn't have. I can't let this curse define me."

I feel the slight flick of her whiskers before she responds. "It already defines you. Being more than it wants you to be is how you resist it. We're all defined by something."

"Indeed, as foolish as this is. I will see you in Vienna, Lorelei."

"Same." She hugs me again and then goes to get her pack. I watch as she hefts it and wave from the porch as she sets out. I wait until she's gone from sight down the lane before I take to my bat form to find the cave.

❧

I awake in darkness. I take a moment to listen to the distant drip of water and the chitter of bats further toward the back. This chamber seems to be too drafty for them. The cave is not particularly comfortable, but it's dark enough. I've been lucky no one has come here these last three weeks, but I cannot assume it will attract no visitors indefinitely.

I get up and fumble with matches to light the lantern. It takes me only two strikes to get it to catch, and I feed it into the lantern to light the wick. Even though I've been living my life in shadow, I still need light to see details. Strange how lantern light and moonlight do no harm to me, but sunlight is deadly.

Here in the cave, I've set up a small camp. I've got my trunk, a lantern, and the lifeless body of Ekrem. Or at least what an outside observer would call a lifeless body.

As promised by Lorelei, the trunk was delivered to the farmhouse. She should be in Vienna by now. I didn't plan to be here for so long, but Ekrem has not recovered. At first I thought he might truly be dead, but slowly he started to heal. It took over a week before I was able to get him to respond enough to feed him. Since then, I've grown confident he's going to recover. I've strewn graveyard dirt under him to ease his rest, taken from the cemetery in Strasek, but I cannot just go steal a coffin. I honestly have no idea if burying a vampire hastens the change or not. So, I've just waited.

I go over and sit down next to him, and gently stroke his forehead. "You're looking better today," I offer.

He doesn't respond at all.

My ears go back, and I take one of his handpaws. "I didn't mean to do this to you," I whisper. "I should have told you no, but I didn't have time to explain it. I didn't have a chance to save you from this."

The paw in my handpaw flinches.

I lean forward. "Ekrem? Ekrem!" I call, squeezing his paw.

His eyes dart behind his closed lids and then they fly open, unfocused, but he blinks. Slowly they converge on me.

"Ekrem?" I say hopefully. While I've been able to nurse him with some blood, he's not been conscious.

"Radic?"

"Oh good, you're ali—" I catch myself. "You're with me."

"Radic," he rasps. "I'm hungry."

I pull him up against me, even if his back is covered in dirt. "I know. You will always be hungry now. You need to fight it."

He shudders. "I feel so hungry, so so hungry." He pauses, obviously noticing how his sense of reality has changed. "You feel this way all the time?"

"With time it has gotten better for me, but it never leaves."

He breaks off from me, suddenly realizing what has happened to him. "You turned me!"

If my heart could still beat, it would catch. "You asked me to."

His mouth opens and closes as he thinks for a moment before he speaks. "I did," he says, looking down and feeling along his chest where the gaping chest wound had been. Already its presence has been erased, and only the shortness of the new fur suggests what happened.

"It will be okay," I whisper, wrapping myself around him. I cradle him against me. He shivers and clings to me, his body cold, lifeless, like mine.

What sin have I committed now? I have doomed Ekrem to eternal emptiness. I have done what I promised myself I never would do.

Yet, as I wipe the tears out of my eyes, I feel the moisture on my paw pads. With awe I notice that for the first time in a hundred years they are not blood, but real tears. Even in this tragedy, I have clawed a little piece of myself back from this curse. I have become just a little bit more alive.

I sob, and let the tears flow freely and squeeze Ekrem to me. "I will protect you, as you protected me. I will teach you how to tread this path silently and unseen."

He whispers, held against me. "Can I control this hunger that gnaws at me?"

"Yes. I did not make you with hate. I will not let you become the monster I was."

"Thank you," he says. I let go of him. He thinks for a moment. "Will I be able to become a bat?"

"I don't see why not, but it takes a bit to understand the form."

"I'd like that. We can fly together under the moon."

"Or course. I would have it no other way."

He takes a breath, even though he doesn't need it anymore. "I understand now how you have suffered. I feel the gnawing on my insides, and yet … I feel content." He looks up at me, his eyes wet with tears, real tears, not bloody tears.

"It's okay," I say, gingerly wiping tears from one of his eyes. I know not how, but he enters into this new life without the rage I carried. "We're in this together."

Afterword

Radic and Ekrem originally appeared in a short erotic story I wrote back in 2019 titled "Loving You is Wrong." Since I enjoyed the characters so much, I decided after finishing that to write a much more detailed and in-depth story involving them. That bloomed into the book you hold in your hands. While I incorporated the original story into this book, I also greatly expanded the setting and character backstories.

The choice to set the story in the Austro-Hungarian Empire comes from wondering about the history of my ancestors who immigrated from the Austro-Hungarian Empire to the United States of America before WWI. Refinement of the draft was provided by my writing group Utunu, Domus Vocis, and Slip-Wolf, who gave me valuable feedback during the drafting process. I must also thank Ty Fox, who hooked me up with an excellent editor, Gabe Foxx. Gabe provided a critical eye for the book as a whole and helped tighten up the narration.

Also, thank you to all my friends who asked me about when the book was coming out, and have been excited to see my second novel get released. I also would like to thank my supporters on Patreon who've stayed with me and kept reading my intermittent updates on the status of the novel. Finally, thank you to my partner Othello Rysingson, who once again pushed me to get the book done and ready in a timely manner. Without him, this wouldn't have been possible. He really does more than he knows.

NightEyes Dayspring, June 2025

About the Author

NightEyes DaySpring is a known troublemaker who is rumored to have a penchant for coffee and an interest in dead, ancient civilizations. He has been writing furry fiction for over twenty years, and over thirty-five of his short stories have been published. His work has appeared in various anthologies, including *Werewolves vs. Fascism*, *Heat*, and *FANG*. He also has contributed multiple stories to *The Voice of Dog* podcast, and he published his first novel, *Scars of the Golden Dancer* in 2022. Currently, NightEyes resides in Florida with his fiancé, where in his spare time he masquerades as an IT professional, plays board games, and doodles.

Visit his website, *nighteyes-dayspring.com*, for more about his writing, or find out where he is on social media at *nighteyes.carrd.co*.